THE
TAKE BACK

BY
STELLA
WALLACE

First paperback edition, May 2019

For those fighting to preserve our dignity.

"My own heroes are the dreamers, those men and women who tried to make the world a better place than when they found it, whether in small ways or great ones. Some succeeded, some failed, most had mixed results... but it is the effort that's heroic, as I see it. Win or lose, I admire those who fight the good fight."

- George R.R. Martin

1. ROAD RUNNER

The dark streets are fetid with human waste and debris tossed aside wantonly, contributing to the piles of rife filth in every direction. The homeless move through the trash heaps they call shelter, dirty blue tarps spread across what started off as a "manageable" tent-ridden shanty town and evolved into grotesque tubes snaking every inch of the sidewalk, stretching out for miles. Many aimlessly wander Skid Row with bellies empty, systems drug-addled, shouting obscenities in Tourette Syndrome-like fashion; others commence to drooling and mumbling to themselves, the day's heat radiating off the concrete zapping what's left of their energy. A jaundiced man in stained clothing holds a porn magazine in one yellowish hand, his grizzled penis in the other.

The misery is desperate and contagious, creating a discourse of hostility with the constant threat of violence hanging heavy in the air. The nasty city soot drains any vibrancy with its tones of industrial brown and warehouse grey. The sirens of emergency vehicles can be heard in the distance, avoiding the conflict found on these streets as a matter of course. It was decided long ago that helping the homeless was too much work simply because there was no money in it.

"The Greatest Depression hit the weakest the hardest. Trillions in debt met with dwindling resources made it impossible to care for those who could no longer help themselves."

A makeshift tent held together by mostly duct tape hosts a middle-aged black woman ravaged by exposure, hunched over, coveting something precious. "Now, I know there's a smidge. I just know it," she murmurs, rocking back and forth, attempting a hit off a hot pipe. She taps it against her head, the pipe singeing her already patchy hair, a scalp scabbed and bleeding from ritual tapping. She hears an uncommon sound for these streets and looks up, spotting something unusual through an opening in the shoddy structure. Peeling back layers, she climbs out, mumbling, "Wha? Wha now?" She shakes her neighbor's equally dilapidated plastic house frantically. "Treese! Girl, look at dis shit. Treese, get out here!"

From above, a dark, living fog of ravenous Asian Tiger mosquitoes fills the air, obscuring the light posts and descending quickly onto street level. Within seconds, the street explodes with pandemonium as those walking the streets of Skid Row scurry for cover, frantic to find shelter. Those already inside their haphazard hovels stumble out to see what the commotion is all about, slapping at their exposed skin as it gets bit from every angle. A naked man wrapped in plastic tries to outrun them, stumbling over a fire hydrant. The plastic flies off as he falls, his eyes rolling into the back of his head as his body seizes, his deafening screams interrupted by vomit erupting from his throat.

The escalated brain swell mimicking a severe case of Encephalitis is killing thousands almost instantly, but not before a great deal of pain and suffering. The cries are drowned out by yet more emergency vehicles in the distance, headed in the opposite direction and away from where they are needed most.

Albert Walker, a slender black man in his fifties, donning a second-hand suit and weathered fedora, is the managing director of the Midnight Mission, the local homeless services charity. Once himself homeless, Albert is still hard at work. He can hear the screams from his desk and springs to the nearest barred window, unable to fully process the carnage playing out before him. The people he swore an oath to help are dying in droves before his eyes.

The mosquitoes inevitably begin to infiltrate the Midnight Mission through the open doors and windows of various rooms, taking more lives with them before their own short life span ends. Albert senses his immediate danger and quickly pries the heating vent from its base, sliding his thin frame into it and replacing the cover, sealing the slats tightly behind him. He narrowly escapes the brutal infestation by using years of acquired street smarts.

A short time later, men in head-to-toe yellow Hazmat suits pressure wash the blood and feces off the sidewalk with brisk precision, as bulldozers push the piles of bodies over to a line of idling garbage trucks. Men from the Command Emergency Relocation Trust, wearing jackets with the CERT logo on them, have closed off the streets with construction safety tape and are rounding up the few remaining survivors from their sealed tents, loading them onto a bus. Entrepreneurs wearing crisp shirts, hard hats, and facemasks move in to survey the orchestrated land grab for immediate development, plans in hand to exploit the bloody catastrophe by building more million dollar one-bedroom apartments. Disaster capitalism in action.

Albert Walker slips out of the heating vent and into an alleyway, undetected, running as fast as he has run since his high school years on the track team.

The sky is a perpetual June Gloom due to the spraying of untold tons of sulfur dioxide to block out natural sunlight in the fight against the threat of global warming. Intense droughts followed. The unnatural splash of the bright green Astroturf breaks up the monotony of the brown hills surrounding the Palos Verdes Golf Club, as the Wounded Hero's Celebrity Golf Tournament is underway. Everyone is grey and ashen except for a famous movie actor with a million-dollar smile, his tan achieved by leisurely hours of fun under the Italian sun sticks out like the faux grass.

Dex Stringer, an accomplished journalist for a notable yet subversive magazine, with the credentials hanging from his neck to prove it, is a powder keg of paranoia. His temperament is less manic and more panic. Standing on the green, slightly apart from the crowd, Stringer carries his disdain on his sleeve. He talks rapidly into a dat recorder. "The hypocrisy of it all. You send a guy six thousand miles away to protect an opium field, I mean fight terrorism, and he comes back in pieces. So, what do you do? You throw him and his fucked-up-forever brothers a golf tournament. Merry fucking Christmas."

He turns to watch Three-Star General Patterson shake hands with the Hollywood contingency, posing for a photo op alongside a soldier with blade runner legs. The soldier takes his turn and the ball goes straight into a sand dune. General Patterson claps, a cigar clenched in his teeth. "You'll get 'em next time!" he offers.

Stringer snaps off a few obligatory shots and scoffs, "Condescending prick."

Nearby, an old vet wearing a sun-bleached 101st Airborne Division cap stares at Stringer. Stringer eyeballs him back. "I'm still on the mailing list from Nam," the old man offers.

"You look like you still have all your parts."

"Claymore took my baby maker in '68 outside Phu Bai." He looks off in the distant with disdain and regret. "I got guys killing themselves every day. I don't see any of them out here playing golf."

The tournament closes out and guests mill about inside the 19ᵗʰ Hole Clubhouse. The A-List celebrities are long gone, but a few B-Listers linger. Holding court at the bar is General Patterson, flanked by uniformed staff members and young vets with adoration in their eyes.

Stringer takes the opportunity to move in when he sees an opening. He sidles up to the bar, joining in on the laughter at one of the General's jokes. As the laughter subsides, Stringer continues to laugh, with a clap of his hands. "Good one, General. Say, General, can you tell us why it is that Command Intelligence directed the whole 9ᵗʰ army to take over the Kandahar province, yet it has no military value? Could it be that we're just there to protect the opium fields?"

The room goes quiet. General Patterson slowly turns to Stringer. "I didn't realize they let civilians in here. I'm sorry, son. What did you say? Something about being thankful? You're welcome," the General sneers and shows him his backside, gritting his yellowed teeth with a hand gesture to have him removed. Two Military Police, or MPs, grab Stringer by the elbows and lead him out of the room.

Stringer struggles as he's being led away, calling out to the young vets in the room, "You think they give a shit about you? You work for drug dealers! When the Taliban had Afghanistan, less than four percent of the world's opium came from that area. Now it's ninety-five percentage! Open your eyes! You're being used!"

"I will gag you!" the MP in charge of removing him threatens.

"With what? Your dick? You'd like that, wouldn't you!"

They hurl him out a back exit. He lands hard and skids on his hands and knees, wincing, not the first time he's been tossed out of a function for causing a ruckus. The MP stands firmly above him, glaring, dissuading him from any further provocation.

The old man is smoking a hand-rolled cigarette nearby. He sidles up, heavy-footed, and stands in between them. "Ok, boys! I'll take it from here. Got the truck parked right over there," he says as he struggles to help Stringer up. "C'mon, buddy. Say goodnight to your new friends. Nighty night." He waggles his fingers towards the officers and steers Stringer towards his vehicle.

As they reach a safe distance from the building, he speaks directly into Stringer's ear in a below-the-radar register. "So, you're the writer who got that joint chief to step down. Man, I read that whole series. How'd you get his staff to open up and admit that shit?"

"Lots of tequila," Stringer says, coughing to catch up to his lost breath.

"I heard what you said to the General. That story's dead as Kennedy. You'll never get anyone on record for that. Too big. Too remote." He helps Stringer into his truck. "I got something for ya, hotshot. Name's Barnaby Lee."

"Dex Stringer. Cheers. Where to, Barnaby?"

Barnaby gets behind the wheel and they drive away without another word.

The 13th Step is a crusty old dive bar overlooking Terminal Island, a port that hosts container and bulk terminals, as well as canneries, shipyards, and Coast Guard facilities. A massive tanker ship and thousands of shipping crates stacked like Legos are within view. Local dockworkers and crusty marina homesteaders greet Barnaby and Stringer as they enter to Stevie Ray Vaughan's Voodoo Child playing faintly on the jukebox. Mabel, the hard bartender in her fifties with gin blossoms on her nose and a tattoo of a lotus flower on her neck, sets up two glasses and pours clear liquid from a nondescript bottle of liquor from behind the bar.

"Hiya, Mabel."

"Hey, Barnaby. We got ice today."

"It's cool. He's with me." Barnaby makes a two-finger salute. The surly bunch of aged, blue-collared retirees share knowing glances and nod in Stringer's direction.

Mabel doesn't miss the chance to rib him, "Who's your girlfriend, Barnaby? Thought you liked 'em thicker."

"Don't get jealous, Mabel. I only have eyes for

you." The sudden flush of his cheeks validates this.

A small television plays in the background. Infamous bad-boy anchorman Reilly Williams, smarmy but polished, leans into camera with a snide tone. "Not a good day to be a heroin addict. Looks like a rash of OD's broke out today on Skid Row due to a bad batch of black tar heroin from Mexico. Stay in school, kids. Drugs are bad. Moving on."

Barnaby and Stringer walk their drinks to a booth by a window facing the harbor and the reflection of the waning sun bathes them in a coppery glow, the boats clanking in the near distance. They look out in time to see a seagull dive straight down into the water to capture an unsuspecting fish.

Barnaby turns to Stringer and looks him square in the eyes before speaking. "You're the kind of mind I want to show something to."

"What fresh hell you got for me today?"

Barnaby takes a stiff swig from his glass. He stretches his lips wide and exhales quickly, making a giddy up sound with the side of his mouth. He lowers his voice. "What you should be printing, what you should really be worried about is the fact that right now, right there, on that dock, is two and half million new vaccines the army has to get to all active personnel by month's end. Why the big rush ya say? They're getting ready to burn the fuckin' forest down, man. And the clock's a ticking."

"Oh, you mean like Ebola?"

"Ebola was a test run. Shit's gonna make Ebola look like a bowl a' cherries." Barnaby takes a hand-rolled cigarette from his breast pocket, lights it, and takes a heavy drag. "I live on disability and boredom. Got nothing better to do but watch them all day long. I make it my business to know when something's not right." He points to a big line of freight carriers being loaded onto trucks. "You can see the West Coast shipment right there. Those containers are like a game of Tetris."

Stringer looks towards the harbor, then back at Barnaby with a look of skepticism. "I'm listening."

"You need to see it up close. It'll all make sense once you see it for yourself." Barnaby downs his drink and shuffles off to settle their tab at the bar, taking his time to flirt with Mabel some more.

Stringer takes out his dat recorder and quietly talks into it. "Afghanistan opium link still undetermined. Following unrelated lead on a large shipment of vaccines for the military. Source is questionable, potentially unreliable. Probably nothing." Stringer stuffs the recording device into his jacket pocket and follows Barnaby out of the bar.

Away from the noise of the bar crowd, the men watch in silence as containers being loaded by automated machines onto trucks boom in the distance. As a clock tower rings in the half-hour, Barnaby points out a forty-foot container with a fan intake on it. "Now, you see, that's weird. The refrigerated ones

16

usually go out in a day or two. That reefer's been sitting for a month, plugged into the dock power supply. And that wouldn't even be the weirdest thing. See how it says Capital on its side? They don't do refrigerator shipping."

He leads Stringer along the pier towards his houseboat, a has-been Mardi Gras style booze cruise with gold and black smokestacks, solar panels, beat up lawn furniture, plants that have been thoroughly cooked by the sun, and a rusted bike hanging upside down off a turret. "This came to me under the wire, from high up. The source is bona fide," he says with a nod. They disappear inside the hull of the musty boat, the steady lilt creating a clanging sound as tackle meets mast.

Once inside, Barnaby beelines for his outdated laptop sitting atop a dark wooden table in the galley. He slips on his reading glasses and opens up a document on the screen. "The tip came in six weeks ago to be on the lookout for an unclaimed refrigerated container. See, they usually go out within forty-eight hours. That one there's been sitting for," he pauses, thinking for a moment, "today makes twenty-eight days. Capital Shipping wasn't even a company until the day before that container arrived, proof of ownership traced back to a one Paradigm Solutions." Barnaby directs him to read his findings.

As Stringer scrutinizes the documents, Barnaby disappears into the kitchen and returns with a stainless steel flask. "Homemade moonshine. Keep away from flame."

Stringer takes a swig and tries not to make a face. He doesn't succeed. "Fresh," he says through puckered lips, handing the flask back.

Barnaby takes notice. "Better yet," he says and pulls out a mortar and pestle filled with white power.

Stringer sees the bowl. "What now?" he asks.

Barnaby kicks at a beat-up tote bag full of prescription pills at his feet. "Oh, a little a' this, a little a' that. Custom blend for tonight. We're going to need maximum focus. And a shit ton of courage." He grabs a brass .308 sniper bullet casing from a collection on the desk and scoops it full of the white powder. "The .22 oughtta be plenty for you." Barnaby tilts his head back and snorts the contents of the bullet.

Stringer hesitates. *Oh, what the hell.* He picks up the smaller bullet shell, dips it into the powder, and follows Barnaby's lead. He's instantly catapulted into a loud miasma of heightened sound and color, then darkness.

A splashing wave wakes Stringer from a blackout. Rubbing his face, he takes a minute to orient himself. Night has fallen and he is rowing a dinghy towards the loading dock, undetected by its skeleton crew. He navigates the boat towards a dark corner and uses his strength to pull himself underneath, tying the small boat to a cleat with a rope found in the bottom of the boat, alongside an army rucksack. Further inspection reveals a penlight, a crowbar, wire cutters, and Barnaby's flask. *For fuck's sake.* He straps the sack to his back to begin the arduous climb up the dock, unseen.

The container is hidden in plain sight among the other containers with names like EVERGREEN and HANJIN and ITALIA. Stringer darts from one shadow to the next, reaching the suspicious container undetected. Clamping the thin penlight between his teeth, he squeezes the lock until it cracks, then uses the crowbar to slowly pry it open. Icy cold air blasts his face. He slips inside, closing the heavy duty Corten steel door behind him. The cooled container is stacked to the rim with sealed packages containing vials labeled "Evomune". Inventory posted on the stainless steel wall reads: Army 507,158 Navy 347,693 Air Force 347,352 Marines 179,762 Total DOD 1,381,965 Coast Guard 41,002 Total Armed Forces 1,422,967 Reserves 1,000,000 Paramilitary 53,000 Total for US Military 2,475,967 Enforcers 1,000,000 = 3.5 million vaccines. He takes pictures of the contents of the crate, as well as the inventory list. A rattling outside freezes his bones.

Barnaby is watching the action from his houseboat through the scope of his M24. A truck rumbles by and parks next to the Capital container. Two men get out of the truck. "Shit," he says and steadies the rifle, aiming for the panel of lights to the left of the crate. His silenced shot misses. "Son of a..." He quickly sets the rifle down and takes a hit off of a small, green bong to steady his nerves. He realigns the meters of his scope, holds his breath, and squeezes another shot. He hits the target, causing the lights to explode as they shatter overhead. The men point and holler, walking over to investigate.

Stringer waits for the noise to pass, staring at the stacks. He pulls out a lockback knife and slices open the packaging from one stack, accesses a vial, and stuffs it in his pocket. He slowly opens one of the double doors. Seeing no one in sight, he high-tails it out of there.

Exiting an automated cab in front of his nondescript hotel, Stringer is anxious to call his editor David Brown, a cocky ladder climber who couldn't make it as a journalist but because of his Daddy's connections was placed in a position to judge other people's work. Always something to prove, David encourages Stringer to take the risks he himself is too afraid to take. It's not his hide in the lion's mouth, but his to be celebrated when a high-profile story comes across his desk.

Stringer scans the parking lot as he fumbles with his key card. No sign of life. He enters his room and retrieves a brand new burner phone from his leather messenger bag hiding under the bed. After several rings, David answers with an irritated tone. "It's getting late. Tell me you have something to print."

"Information is my bastion."

"The line's secure."

"David, I'm onto something big with pictures and a sample to prove it. They're in a big hurry to vaccinate all military. Protection from some gnarly virus. They know something's coming and it's going to be nationwide."

"Holy shit. Where are you?"

"I'm at my hotel. I'm going to bang out this story and catch the red-eye. It'll be in modusCloud first thing."

"Watch your six, man," David says and hangs up. The swank interior of David's New York City apartment, albeit small, glows from the lights of the skyscrapers surrounding his building. From the same phone, he dials a number from memory and speaks flatly into the phone. "David Brown for Comptroller 684F23. Yes, I'll hold." David stares out the window at the even taller, shinier skyscraper under construction across the street. "Goodbye, one bedroom," he says with a sinister leer.

Stringer works furiously at his laptop from the standardized desk in his room. He gets up to pace the floor, deep in thought, sporadically scanning through the photos of the refrigerated vaccines from his camera. He hears a sound and stops in his tracks.

The ominous whirring comes from the other side of his hotel window. He peers out from behind the closed curtains to see the beady, red flashing lights of an Enforcer Drone hovering just outside his room. He drops to the floor and unplugs the lamp. "Shit. Shit! David, you sellout, greedy motherfucker!"

He quickly gathers his things and emerges from his room on all fours, his leather bag strapped across his chest. He uses the support beams of the hotel's second floor as shields, finding a walkway that leads to the back of the building. He hears the buzzing sound of the drone closing in behind him. He makes a run for it.

Delilah sits idly by in her beat-up cab on the side of the road adjacent to a shoddy park, waiting for her next ride request to come in. She masks the beauty she inherited from her Cubana mother with a Greek fisherman's cap to cover her long, black hair, fingerless driving gloves, and raw attitude. Navigating through the harsh freeways of the vast metropolis requires a level grit fit for a warrior.

A well-dressed older man walks by with his pedigree dog, shouting into his cell phone. "It's got to be ready for the show! There's no ifs, ands, or buts! They agreed to a delivery date by the end of the week. Here it is, the twenty-first. Are you hearing me? Is this thing on?"

The expertly coiffed animal strains to relieve himself as the man ignores it, pulling on the leash and subsequently trailing a thin line of excrement behind.

An Enforcer, heavily clad in black militarized gear, steps out from behind a tree and withdraws a tactical security baton meets Maglite flashlight from his utility belt. In his other hand is a biometric device that uses facial recognition to instantly identify and process people without probable cause. People argued it was like playing god, but it was too late. Civil liberties were a thing of the past. The newer generations would never know that search warrants, court orders or due process were ever things.

The Enforcer shines the searing beam of the Maglite into the man's face. "Dennis Hodges?"

The man shields his eyes, exasperated. "What!"

"Sir, you've neglected to clean up after your animal. West Hollywood City Statute eleven seventy-four states it's a violation of health code 186. A private animal owner is responsible for pet waste. That's an immediate $1,000 fine. Failure to comply will result in animal destruction." The Enforcer takes a step forward.

The man points to the tiny piece of poo produced by the show dog. "For that? Are you fucking serious right now?"

"Sir, please refrain from using such language or I will be forced to fine you for insubordination."

"You would kill my dog?"

"The law's the law, sir."

The man talks into his phone. "Steve, I have to call you back. I have an Enforcer trying to squeeze me over here." The man hangs up his phone. "I don't have that kind of cash on me! This is ridiculous! I don't suppose you take credit cards?"

"As a matter of fact, we do." The Enforcer produces a handheld wireless credit card processing solution device from his utility belt.

The man pulls out his wallet and reluctantly hands him a card, shaking. "Unbelievable!"

The Enforcer takes it and swipes it into the machine, printing out a thermal paper receipt.

Del watches the event unfold through the viewfinder of her phone as she records the exchange. She ends the recording and immediately begins uploading it to the encrypted Fair Play app. The upload is interrupted by an alert.

A monotone female voice says, "Task notification. You have a new intercepted ride request. Accept or deny." She accepts it with the push of a button. The voice continues, "Task engaged. Proceed to route." Del pulls away from the curb towards the pickup address on her screen.

Three girls dressed to the nines, phones in hand, pile into the cab. One of the girls notices Del. "Hey, you're not an automated driver!"

"System's down. If you want to wait for it to be restored, no problem." She motions to cancel the ride, knowing full well the response. The layoffs after automation were severe. This song and dance is all part of the ruse to keep actual drivers employed and on the road.

The girl stops her. "No, that's fine. We have somewhere we have to be."

Del pushes the button on her device to signify the start of the ride and proceeds to their destination. The girls cluck away from the backseat until one squeals, "Live feed!" The girls instantly stop talking and focus on their phone screens.

Frankie Q, a sexually ambiguous rock-n-roller with dark curls and manicured facial hair, steps into the frame of his walk-in closet, the backdrop a line of colorful clothes and scarves of multiple prints. He has that just-rolled-in-the-hay look with his smudged eye makeup and sweaty sheen. He reaches behind him and grabs a leopard print silk robe, tying it around his lithe, bare midriff in a dainty bow. "Hi-eeee! Welcome to Frankie Q's Closet. I luh you!"

The girls respond in unison, "I luh you!"

Del peers back at them in her rearview mirror and eye rolls deeply.

"Listen up, slaves. Time to double down. Take a selfie with a real-life homeless person and you'll double your daily points on Topp App. This is for all of you who slept in, like me! You have one hour. Byeee!"

One of the girls yells, "Driver! Stop the car!" She grabs the handle of the car door and starts to open it. "What the fuck," Del utters, pulling the car over as the girl jumps and runs towards a young black man passed out on the sidewalk, his shirt riding up his back, exposing his scabby skin.

Her friends cry out from the back of the car,

"Kelsey! Be careful!"

Kelsey crouches down next to him to take a selfie. "Oh my god! He stinks!"

Del shakes her head in disgust. She clears the screen on her device and opens a live photo of a six-year-old boy running clumsily along a well-worn path in the woods. A woman's hand enters the live photo's frame holding a dandelion clock. She blows the filamentous achenes from the dandelion into the air to the pure delight of the little boy. "Make a wish," the woman says off camera. The little boy turns his face towards the sky and giggles, throwing his hands in the air to catch them. When the live photo ends, Del exhales and restarts it.

The homeless man rolls over on his cardboard platform and makes a gruff sound. Kelsey shrieks and runs back to the car, climbing in and slamming the door. She frantically rummages through her bag. "Where's the hand sanitizer?"

Her friends are chanting, "Post it! Post it!"

Kelsey is visibly shaken. "Oh my god, he was so gross, you guys." She smears her hands with the found sanitizer. She looks at the photo. "Ew! I look like a horse face killer!" she cries and immediately uploads the photo. A voice on her device says, "Task verification complete. Topp App Participation points 500."

Moments later, they arrive at a trendy restaurant rife with eager valet attendants. She waves them off, pointing to her passengers getting out behind her. She ends the fare and the voice on her device says, "Task complete. Total Topp App Citizenship points 9832."

Del replies with a snicker, "Thanks, Sheila. Why don't you take five and go get yourself a cup of coffee." She pulls out into traffic.

At a traffic light, Del stares blankly ahead, awaiting the green. The music on the radio is especially slow and sad, yet she remains steely-eyed. As the light changes, she begins to move through the intersection.

Her back door suddenly opens and a frantic looking Dex Stringer gets in. If he was manic before, he's now downright ballistic. "Car for Dex?"

"Hey, buddy!"

"How ya doin' tonight? Good? You good?"

Del looks back at him for a moment, sizing him up. "I'm alright. What the fuck's up with you?"

"Right. Good. Listen, I gotta get to the airport. LAX. United." He fumbles with the power window, gets it to lower, and looks up at the sky with a furrowed brow.

Del starts the ride and weaves through the thick traffic. A car honks behind them loudly, startling Stringer. "Jeez! How do you drive in LA? I abandoned my car years ago, never looked back. It got so bad I'd have to burn my arm with a cigarette to make a left turn. You're like a ninja."

Her response is deadpan. "I'm a Zen Buddhist monk master."

"Right. You can't control anything. You accept everything and nothing at the same time. You are completely part of something you can't touch or effect. What an illusion, huh. So much is spiralling out of control. None of it makes sense. And we're forced to accept it and be ok with it. Because what choice do we have, right?" He checks the sky again. "Did you know we're hurtling through the universe at thirty-three thousand miles per hour? Control is truly subjective."

"Tell that to the Order."

His leg begins to twitch. "It's not about bread and circuses anymore. It's the Roman Senate all over again! What do you think their reaction's going to be when eighty percent of the population is replaced by technology?"

"Tell me about it," she says under her breath.

"It doesn't even have to be armed conflict anymore. We're talking cyber warfare. The engineering of a financial nine eleven. It's happening, you know."

"You take your meds today?"

"Ok, let's just say, for instance, you're China's central bank and you hold two trillion in US debt. You're looking to surpass the US as the Global hegemon. You have the gravitas to begin lending the yuan at a highly discounted rate to other countries. If they effectively replace the dollar en masse, the dollar is devalued greatly. Your ally in this, Russia, underwrites the whole thing with their untapped natural resources. So, you're in a very powerful position, yes? You can squeeze the Federal Reserve into a more favorable position. Believable, right?"

"I don't know, man. As far as I knew, we're China's biggest consumers. It wouldn't behove them to render us inoperable, now would it."

"Astute observation, but not if their end game is to replace the New York Stock Exchange. And China is totally committed. They're like a petulant little six-year-old with a flamethrower and they're going to burn the whole house down." Stringer sweeps the sky. "Hey, what's your name?"

"Del."

"Dex Stringer here. Hey Del, you notice any Enforcer Drones overhead? I think they're tracking me. My editor sold me out."

"You must be very important." She glances up at the sky.

"Fucking illegal surveillance. People grew too complacent to do anything about it. Complicity and control. That's their game. I've got them dead to rights. I uncovered a treasure trove of vaccines they're storing for all military personnel. I'm going to bust this story wide open before they have a chance to follow through on whatever diabolical plan they have in mind. Sure, they'll try to spin it. But there's something sticky about the truth. It really, really wants attention."

She spots an Enforcer Drone through the trees.

It appears to be hovering above them, unhinging her. "Not to further the freakout, but I think that's the drone you're looking for."

"Shit! It's not the phone. They can't be tracking me unless I'm tagged. How could I have been tagged? Fuck!"

"And the hits keep coming."

Traffic comes to a full stop, signalling a check-point up ahead. Enforcers flank the southbound lanes of the 110 Freeway.

Stringer sees this and erupts. "Motherfucker! This is it! I can't let them take me! The public needs to know this is a setup!" Stringer jumps out of the back of the cab, slaloming through dozens of idling cars, a few honking their horns in surprise. He reaches the previous exit ramp and disappears under the overpass.

Enforcers zealously interrogate every vehicle. As Del's cab approaches the checkpoint, she retrieves a clear plastic bag tucked under her visor above her head containing the necessary paperwork. She cracks her window, slides it out so it dangles within reach, and seals the window back up, locking her doors.

A strapping Enforcer with dashing good looks, Richie Wick, flags Del to stop. He bends down and asks through the window, "How we doing tonight?"

She looks forward, avoiding eye contact. "I don't answer questions."

"Is there some reason you can't roll down your

window?"

"I don't answer questions."

Richie looks amused. "You don't answer questions?"

"Am I being detained?"

"Is there a reason why I should detain you?"

"I don't answer questions. Am I being arrested? Am I free to go?"

"I'm not sure how to answer that." Richie points a facial recognition device at her. The dossier that pops up reads, "Do not detain. Clearance Level 3." He leans in to make eye contact with her. She continues to stare straight ahead. He circles her vehicle, pulling out a track patch and sticking it out of sight under her license plate. He circles back and gives her car a pat. "Ok, have a nice night."

She responds by stepping on the gas. As she drives off, he thinks *Who are you, little Miss Delilah?* He files the number of the tracking patch into the system, makes a printout of the information, and stuffs it in his shirt pocket. He flags down the next car.

Del peers out her rearview mirror, checking out Richie's physique, her gaze lingering. She exhales deeply and exits the freeway.

After driving aimlessly around for a few blocks, she spots a man behind the wheel of a stopped truck, looking distraught. She rolls down her window. "Battery?" she asks.

"It has a breathalyzer and Daddy was thirsty."

He exits the truck and sways his way into in her cab. "Alright! Let's get out of here!" He makes a call and speaks loudly into his phone. "No no, two Russians girls. The acro batty ones. And a Thai girl. That massages." There's a pause. "Special costumes? I don't know. Can they dress as Valkyries?" There's a pause on the other end of the line. "Like shield maidens. I have my own video stuff. Just the three is fine. Thanks, Mitzy. I really appreciate this. Love you too, baby." He hangs up.

"What, no midgets?"

The guy laughs. "No, that was last week. Here's the link." He hands her a business card. She adds it to the useless pile of cards in her middle console.

They arrive at his house and he trips getting out of the car, jumps up on two feet, and sticks the landing. "Cowboy up! You see that? Six years of Krav Maga." Before shutting the door, he notices something on the floor of the back of her cab. He picks it up. "Is this your thingy?"

"Ah, shit. I guess that means it's not your thingy."

"Nope. I have all my thingies." He passes the object to her, shuts the door clumsily, and stumbles inside his house. She stares at the object for a moment, unsure of what she's looking at, then slides it into her bag and moves on.

It's late and the Sunset Strip in Hollywood is crackling with action. Scantily clad women woefully balance on itty-bitty shoes, while men play out their

Peter Pan syndrome. As Del scouts for fares, her vision is eclipsed by a gigantic electronic billboard spewing advertisements for Topp App. An image flashes of a woman carrying an armful of groceries, turning to the camera and flashes a toothy smile. A guy getting a loan from a bank gives a big thumbs up. A woman's voice, overtly smooth and robotic in its delivery, accompanies the images. "A better you, achieved through consistency and stability. Work hard. Get what you want out of life. Improve your score on Topp App today."

Del shuttles a drunk couple in the middle of a fight over their inability to buy a house and start a family because of their outrageous student loan debt. She drops them off across town in Silver Lake, checks the time, and engages her CB radio. "This is Road Runner. Looking for a taco date on Lemoyne. Any takers? Over."

A voice responds in a thick Armenian accent, "Road Runner! It is Smokey the Bandit. I am ten away only. I am happy to be your taco date."

The gentrified, late-night crowd commingles seamlessly with the Norteño music being piped out of the food truck. Del and Smokey lean against the wall of a closed storefront, awaiting their handmade tacos.

Smokey pulls out a cigar and hands it to her. "Cuban!"

She smiles and slides it in her pocket. She fetches a handful of individually wrapped chocolates from her other pocket and fills his cupped hands with them. His face lights up.

An old Mexican woman stands on the side of the road, selling bouquets of fresh-picked flowers. An Enforcer stops her and asks her for her ID and a permit to sell. She does not comprehend his request and attempts to move along. The Enforcer grabs her by her long, black ponytail and slams her to the ground, resting the full weight of his large frame on her soft body. She cries out in pain. A second Enforcer walks up, grabs the flower bunches from the ground, and shreds them, the red petals flying in every direction. The first Enforcer handcuffs the woman as she breaks down sobbing.

Onlookers watch, infuriated, as Del records it and uploads it the Fair Play app. When their tacos arrive in the window of the food truck, they don't have much of an appetite.

Smokey's phone alerts another ride request. "Rent next week. I must take this. Stay strong, Road Runner. Don't let these bastards get to you." He makes his way to his parked cab.

Del takes out the cigar, bites off the end, and lights it. As she watches the Enforcers cart off someone's querida abuela, she gets a notification from her news feed. The screen reads: Avoid Highland Avenue from Santa Monica to Wilshire Boulevard due to a single car accident resulting in a fatality. She scrolls down and sees a picture of Dex Stringer plastered below the article. She reads aloud in disbelief. "Noted independent news media journalist Dex Stringer last seen speeding on Highland Avenue at 4:32 am. His car collided with a tree and he was killed instantly. No further details at this time."

She switches over to the Fair Play app and scans for content. She finds a video of a bystander at the scene. "It was weird, man. Like all of a sudden, this guy was hauling ass. Then it was like, boom! A huge explosion. And then the car, it like flew, and hit that tree. Crazy man. The engine's way over there." The guy points to a chunk of charred metal thirty feet in the opposite direction of the tree.

The feed is interrupted by a high-pitched alarm from on her phone, accompanied by a red flashing light. Prep Egress, a security app, notifies her that someone has approached her home that does not have clearance to be there. The app asks if she would like for the Enforcers to be called in. She presses DENY, stubs out the cigar, pockets it, and hurries to her car. She peels out, weaving deftly through traffic, running fresh red lights.

The sun is just starting to rise as Del silently enters her front door. She hears the sound of a man's voice and takes a .357 Beretta from her waist, holding it straight out in front of her body. She steps into her living room and sees an astute looking man sitting on the couch next to her son, the boy from the live picture. Wise beyond his years, Bodhi is the kind of child that if he ever got lost, he'd be found in town communing with the elders. The two are engaged in a card game.

Valentina, Del's ravishing mother, looks on from the other side of the room, dotingly. Del's hand is steady, aiming the pistol at the man's head. "Who the fuck are you and what are you doing in my house?"

The man looks up nonchalantly. "He is a most extraordinary boy," the man says gently.

Del turns to Valentina. "Mother, take Bodhi into the bedroom."

"Del, honey, this is Leland Djinn. He works with…"

"Do it. Now!"

"Oh, Del. Is this necessary?" Valentina takes Bodhi's hand and exits the room quietly, mouthing the word "Sorry" to Leland.

"Who the fuck are you?"

"Bishop sent me."

Del shakes her head. "Fuck that guy."

"We've tracked John Mills. We need your help. The boy, too."

Del slowly lowers the gun. "John?" She gapes at him, thrown. "He's dead."

"It's bigger than you imagine."

Del packs snack food into her bag, grabbing a handful of coffee beans and stuffing them in her pocket for good measure. Valentina dresses Bodhi for

the road trip ahead, wrapping herself in a beige rua-
na. She turns and gives Del a steady look. "We knew
this day would come."

"Did we though?" she replies sardonically. Bodhi
gazes up at her with a peaceful, loving look. She softens. "You ready for an adventure?" Bodhi smiles.

Leland is waiting on the front steps as Del, Valentina and Bodhi join him outside. Del surveys the
street, as well as the sky. There is nothing out of the
ordinary. They climb into Del's cab and hit the road.

The drive is silent, mostly, but for the sound of
Del crunching on coffee beans and the soft pulse of
the beacon signal from the long-range tracking device
Leland holds in the passenger seat next to her, guiding
the way.

Valentina and Bodhi sit in the backseat playing
Where in the World. With each passing car, Bodhi
names the brand. "That is a Mazda," he says.

"Where in the world does a Mazda come from?"

"Japan." The next car comes along. "That one is
a Merk…"

"Mercedes."

Bodhi looks up at his Grandmother with spar-
kling eyes. He looks out and sees another. "That one
is a Volvo and it comes from Sweden," he says quickly,
beating her to the question. She takes his hand in hers
and squeezes it tightly.

"Gene modification had slowly stripped food of proper nutri-

tion. Babies born on the spectrum became commonplace. The world was tough enough, even without a unique child to care for. People stopped wanting to procreate because the heartbreak was too great. No one could afford it anyway. The system was designed this way. The messages were laid clear. And the people followed."

The car heads east on the 10 Freeway, the long stretch of open desert road unfolding in front of them an invitation to make a distant memory of the dirty city behind them.

"I didn't know John well. It was just the one time. But there was something about him that made me want to hold onto that growing baby in my belly. Bodhi held on, too. He is the greatest boy I've ever known. He has compassion that transcends his age every year that passes, in a world that has grown unsympathetic. Somehow, he still believes in magic. And it's my job to protect him with my life."

The cab travels along a dusty road in the middle of the Sonoran Desert, the sun high in the sky scorching the barren earth below. Passing the colorful Salvation Mountain, a small shed touts a sign welcoming them to Slab City. Del looks in her rearview mirror and sees another sign on the opposite side of the structure that reads "Question Everything", accompanied by a painted eyeball, staring her down.

As the car makes its way through an empty canvas

of dehydrated vegetation, structures made from odd materials pop up amongst the run-down RVs, multi-colored painted buses with no wheels, and a plethora of burnt-out vehicles. Art pieces from refurbished garbage pepper the landscape. A dead tree hosts dozens of worn sneakers, dangling from its brittle branches. Another sign reads "The Last Free Place in America", offering a makeshift sitting area comprised of beat up couches, discolored chairs, and ramshackle metal structures.

The atmosphere screams quiet desolation. Nothing living is in sight under the punishing sun, but for the birds of prey circling overhead. Leland follows the tracker through the windy dirt roads. They stop in front of a surprisingly well-manicured plot, the area adroitly fenced in. A white pickup truck parked for easy access, water tanks that appear full, massive solar panels, and sufficient shade structures betray someone with a broad skill set lives here. A sign on the front gate reads "Forget beware of dog. Beware owner," with a picture of a gun pointed directly at the reader. An American flag dances in the wind.

"He's here," Leland says, looking up from the tracking device. Del slowly pulls the car up and parks it. Leland climbs out.

"Bodhi, stay put," Del says firmly, looking to her mother to enforce it. She gets out and follows Leland.

A windmill sits atop metal scaffolding behind the living quarters. Through the haze of the heat, a rugged man is repairing the base of one of the sails. John Mills turns when he hears the car's arrival. He is covered in tattoos, a thousand-yard stare in his eyes.

A yellow-haired girl with a deep scar across her face pulls up on a dilapidated bike with a banana seat. She gives Del and Leland a quick wave. Mills descends the scaffolding, plucking something from a nearby chest and covering it in plastic before walking towards the little girl. "How many did we get today, Lucy?" he asks.

She retrieves items from her basket wrapped in burlap, revealing four eggs and guava. He hands her a large block of ice and she places it in her basket. "Tell your mother I said thank you," he says and she pedals off with a wave.

Leland is sizing up the machine Mills built, a system that pulls water from the humidity in the air and collects it into a plastic bin, using the windmill for energy. "Wow, Milly. You've really made something of this," he says, the compliment resonating in his voice.

"Ice is civilization," Mills says, barely above a whisper.

Del's approach is filled with trepidation. She is disarmed by John's appearance, the man in front of her a hardened shell of the man from her memories.

Before Valentina can stop him, Bodhi jumps out of the car and takes off running. Del tries to stop him. "Bodhi, wait!"

The boy doesn't stop. He continues to run towards Mills, only stopping when he gets within a few feet from him. He looks up at Mills and smiles. *I saw you in my dreams. You look exactly how I pictured you.*

Mills drops to his knees. "I'm your Dad, aren't I."

Bodhi nods. John wraps his arms around him and hugs him.

Del covers her mouth with one hand, staving back tears. Mills catches Del's eyes and stands. Bodhi takes his hand and they walk together towards her.

"I didn't want to put you in danger," he says softly.

"Well, here we are!" The bite to her tone cuts the air sharply, the fresh tears telling a different story. "Glad you're not dead. The tattoos are a nice touch. Do you play in a band, too?"

Mills nearly cracks a smile. He looks to Leland. "How did you find me?"

"Bishop has always known where you are. You're his most valued asset and your particular skill is required at present. It's time to get these bastards."

Mills closes his eyes and takes a deep breath.

The Nest is located beneath a facility in the high desert of Southern Nevada, an hour north of Las Vegas. It is camouflaged by the largest government-controlled land parcel in the country, occupied by the Intelligence Gathering Agency, or IGA, a heavily guarded compound created to control the supremacy of the Order, using terrorism as an excuse to collect

41

electronic intelligence data globally. The Nest was formed to counter the IGA's economic and social control and as far as anyone is concerned, it does not exist.

As the car approaches the locked swinging barricade, they pass a small airfield where an unclassified fleet of untraceable Janet planes arrive and depart throughout the day.

"John was a part of a government operation that has been hidden for decades and for good reason. It should never have happened at all. This operation was created in the name of National Security, but it quickly became a black operation kept secret from the American people. Until now." Leland hands them lanyards with their photos on them. "This will get you behind the curtain." They pass through the manned security gate and are directed to park the cab in what looks to be a simple, nondescript warehouse.

A young MP leads them into the main base of operations for the IGA, a spacious office employing thousands of agents. The center of the room is filled with desks pointed towards various monitors, a set of large displays wrap around multiple consoles with servers covering the length of the walls. Office and board rooms surround the outer ridge. Steps lead to other computer stations and additional walls lined with servers.

The MP quickly ushers them to the far end of the office, through a back corridor, and into a small

elevator. There is a sign on the wall that says "No surveillance past this point". The MP falls out of line as
he does not have proper clearance.

The elevator has a control switch that requires a
thumbprint and a retinal scan to access the sublevels.
Leland initiates access and they descend. The doors
open on a dark hallway leading to the Nest's high-
tech main headquarters with the most advanced com-
munications and imagery available, run by a band of
hand-picked IT geniuses and internet denizens called
the Amorphous Cell, sentinels with an eye on the
world. The internet's first army, their network extends
outside the office, operating in their day-to-day lives
across the globe through an encrypted network, at the
ready to procure Intel on any matter pertaining to exposing the truth.

Their normal frat boy humour is eclipsed by the
pressing updates, but not before Amir Chirya, a tech-
whiz kid from Pakistan and a Harvard research fellow
conducting studies on political corruption, whispers
to another with a jab and a point of his finger. "Holy
shit. That's John Mills!"

Leland makes the introductions. "Del, John, Valentina, and Bodhi, this is the Amorphous Cell, where
sacrifice for the greater good is our first and last name.
Amir is the only moonlighter here, assisting Bishop
upstairs at the IGA, as well as down here in the Nest,
under the radar. The rest of these brilliant nerds live
here full time. Stay away from their quarters if you

care about your olfactory sense."

A pot-bellied Asian hacker, called Fu for his Fu Manchu, does his best Vader. "Come to the Dark Side, Luke."

"Recent events have brought us here, our individual roles to follow. Amir, I believe you have pressing news?"

Amir clears his throat. "We believe something has been set into motion, yes. Is it okay if I…"

"Yes, everyone here has been cleared." Leland nods his approval.

The group is told to gather around a monitor projecting a viral video that has recently emerged. As they approach the terminal, Amir explains, "This was recorded live yesterday afternoon on Fair Play, an app that sends a live feed to an underground Civil Liberties Union server via the Darknet that creates instant viral videos by sending content to the millions who securely subscribe and dedicated to ensuring the video won't get taken down by the Order."

They watch as the video begins in what looks to be a public library. Albert Walker from the Midnight Mission is sitting at a computer terminal, glancing nervously from side to side, as if he is expecting detection at any minute. He appears rattled. "I saw what happened on Skid Row with my own eyes. Mosquitoes, man. Thousands of 'em! Took everybody out. It wasn't a bad batch of heroin like the news keeps reporting." He hears a commotion coming towards him and stands up, putting his hands on his head. "Son, I'm sorry. I made mistakes and ended up on the street. But I turned it around, son, and gave back to my community best I could. Sorry you couldn't forgive me." He fights back tears as a group of heavily armed Enforcers come up from behind him and beat him with tactical security batons. He crumples to the ground. They pick him up and an Enforcer approaches the computer. He pushes a button, shouting, "Motherfucker!" before the video goes black.

The room is silent. Amir pulls up additional footage on the monitor. "We were able to procure this off of an IP CCTV security camera from an old pawnshop across the street from the Mission. My guess is they missed it in the sweep of all surveillance. That CERT arrived before any law enforcement confirms this was a set-up," he says squarely, playing the footage. The screen shows South San Pedro Street at night, the wandering homeless ominously lit from a beam of light provided by the shoddy light pole from above. It suddenly grows dark, as a massive swarm of mosquitoes descend, eclipsing the beam.

Fu calls attention to his monitor. "I've been tracking the garbage trucks from ground zero. They were refueled along the way, without stopping, highly unusual and suspect, and arrived at your favorite criminal franchise and mine, Paradigm Solutions. Hidden below the tangled brush of the Archuleta Mesa at the Dulce Base in New Mexico." He opens satellite feed of the garbage trucks disappearing one by one into the wide mouth of a secret laboratory buried within a foreboding mountainside.

They watch as a black helicopter lands in a clearing attached to the facility. Private security personnel are there to greet the dark figure disembarking. Mills recognizes him immediately. He is not happy. "Snakes. I hate snakes."

"B.D. Blackwell," Leland offers.

Del is trying to make sense of all this. She looks around the room and sees a wall with pictures of men and women stuck to it. The sign above reads "Our Fallen". She is surprised to see Dex Stringer among them, the glue still drying on his photo. "Hey, what are the odds? I had this guy in my cab last night. He was acting cagey." She rummages through her bag. "This slipped out of his pocket when he high-tailed it out of my cab at a checkpoint. He said they were after him because of some military vaccines he discovered." She hands the object over to Leland. It's the vial labeled "Evomune".

Lieutenant Colonel Joseph Bishop walks into the room, wearing a Tibetan monk shirt, with brass fobs and loops across the front. He holds an ornate, teak box in his hands. The room falls quiet. He walks around the room meeting everybody's eyes while offering the contents of the box: Figs.

He starts with Leland, who takes a fig immediately with an obedient nod of his head.

Mills is next. Never losing eye contact, Mills takes two and pops them in his mouth with a smirk.

When Bishop gets to Bodhi, he reaches down and tussles the boy's hair. Bodhi smiles, takes a fig, and says, "Thank you, Grandpa."

Valentina reaches demurely for the box. Bishop takes her wrist and smells it. "Your superior genes haven't let you down, Tina," he hums.

Her cheeks reflect the hue of sunset. "My dove."

Del is last, standing with her arms defiantly crossed. Bishop closes the lid and hands the whole box to her. She rolls her eyes and takes it reluctantly.

He turns to face the room, his cadence measured. "B.D. Blackwell holds lucrative contracts in for-profit reconstruction and blanket surveillance, courtesy of the IGA, operating outside any government oversight. A dealer of influence, arms, and commodities, the reason we invade countries is to benefit people like Blackwell and his friends. They create fake enemies in the name of Defense to fight fake wars so they can take all the money right out from under our noses. A silent war against the people.

"But it's not the money that interests him. He is the consiglieri for the Rotterdam Clan, a family that has independently controlled the world's financial market for over two hundred years. In order to engineer the world's economy in their favor and maintain their stronghold, it was necessary for them to create a science of control over all economic factors. Their

47

monopoly was established by controlling the planet's raw materials and manipulating the public into a system of slave labor, suppressing the people from building lasting connections between economics and other energy sciences.

"Blackwell thrives off of this power to control others, to make big moves for the Order so he can be made to feel like one of them. The world will remain entrenched in their sovereignty until the Order is isolated and removed from power.

"When I began this fight, I couldn't have dreamed the size of their greed, or how many people would be affected by it. Sacrifices have not gone unnoticed." He gives his wife a tender look. "It's always been a question of timing. This is our time. No one else has this opportunity. Let no one take it away from us.

"We have no real idea what we're up against, or the lengths they will continue to go. What we do know is that they've damaged our Earth long enough. It's time to end their reign."

2. An Eye for Psi

A Boeing 757 aircraft hummed along nicely, reaching altitude with the bong of the seatbelt sign, the thrum of the engine wrapped passengers in a soft sound blanket. An adorable little girl began kicking the seat of an angry businessman having to fly coach in front of her. "So sorry," the mother said, throwing down her magazine to attend to the child.

The little girl looked out the window and said, "Mummy look! There's a little plane in the sky!"

"Of course, honey. It's called air traffic." The mother slid the window shade down, handed her daughter a coloring book, and retrieved her magazine.

The captain's overtly calm voice came on over the intercom. "Ladies and gentlemen, this is your captain speaking. We're being rerouted to Fort Detrick in Frederick as a security precaution. Nothing to worry about, folks. Just sit tight and we'll be back on our way in no time."

The plane broke right and the "little plane", a fighter jet, continued on the plane's original path.

As the Director of the Aeromedical Isolation Team stationed at Fort Detrick, Major Joseph Bishop and his men were positioned on the tarmac, suited up in white Hazmat suits. There were countless emergency vehicles surrounding their formation. Bishop's expression was solemn as he watched the plane touch ground.

A crackling came through Bishop's radio, followed by, "Strategic Command Center for Major Bishop."

"Go for Bishop."

"Biochemical threat. Deadly virus onboard. End Zone One ordered."

Bishop struggled to speak. "Why aren't we conducting a quarantine?"

"Contagion does not warrant a quarantine. This is a National Security issue. Command, please confirm the order."

"Confirmed. End Zone One ordered," he choked.

The only female member of his team looked on, dismayed. "Guess this means it's not a drill."

A towbarless tug positioned two low-level arms on either side of the aircraft nose landing gear, engaging the aircraft gear leg and raising it slightly off the ground. After the ground crew team ensured that no part of the aircraft structure would impact any fixed object, vehicle, or other aircraft, the aircraft was towed into an enormous hangar. After coming to a complete stop, the ground crew team accessed the external control panel to cut the power and thus communication to the plane.

The people on board looked around nervously, the only interior light coming from the emergency exit and aisle beacons, the bioluminescent lighting casting an orange glow on their faces. The sound of the clunky machinery being manipulated outside the plane put them further on edge.

The businessman turned around to the little girl who started to whimper. "They're just fixing something on the plane, little one. It'll be fine."

The sudden oxygen masks descending from the ceiling of the plane, along with an incessant bong bong bong, startled the little girl and she began to wail. Her mother instinctually put on her own mask, helping the little girl with her mask next.

A seasoned flight attendant resorted to her calm, but firm, emergency mode. "Ladies and gentlemen, please remain seated. The flight crew will come around to help you shortly." She fulfilled her duty that day to quickly attend to the others.

After getting the go-ahead from Bishop, a team member opened the valve connected to the plane's oxygen intake and blasted the interior with poisonous Sarin gas.

The ground crew forever heard the shattering screams, as bodily functions failed. The cries turned silent as the twitching passengers onboard slowly asphyxiated, their ability to control the muscles involved in breathing lost.

The plane was scrubbed, the lifeless bodies incinerated. Small parts of the dematerialized aircraft were hauled onto a freighter and deposited out to sea.

"The Intel came from up on high: A class 5 Emergency Airborne Event. National security was top priority and all precautions were taken to protect the ground. We were told a biochemical weapon had been released on that flight and the people on board were already dead and didn't know it. I was supposed to feel like a hero that day. I didn't feel like a hero. We were used. We were used and we were lied to."

B.D. Blackwell's office, located in the Department of Security building in Langley, Virginia, was sparsely furnished barring a Zoffoli Minerva Globe containing ornate crystal bottles of scotch and a set of mounted Texas Longhorns behind his head.

Bishop stormed in. "What did I just do? That plane was nowhere near the Pentagon! You falsified a contagion!"

"What, no salute?" Blackwell remained seated, peering up from his desk. "You did what was asked of you. For your actions, you are to be promoted to Lieutenant Colonel. And you are not to speak of this to anyone. Is that understood?"

"Innocent people were killed. I have blood on my hands, Goddamn you!"

"This is a DoS matter. Your crew has been eliminated from further review." Blackwell pulled from his desk a folder containing images of the dead bodies of Bishop's team members. One depicts a man hanging from a rafter. Another, the woman, shot in the head, twice, gun in hand. Both suicided.

"Time stood still and my rage was so white hot the only thing I could see was my smashing his windpipe in an instant. But I knew it would all be in vain because they would find and kill me."

"We appreciate the work you did on the Starseed program. We'd like to see it continued. Strictly classified." A photo stares up at them from the jacket cover of a book sitting on Blackwell's desk, an eccentric looking man wearing an ascot and smoking a cigar. "Go find him and bring him back."

Bishop couldn't feel his limbs. "He'll never come."

Blackwell stood and handed him his orders. "Respect the hand that feeds."

"And then the clarity of it all set it in. I knew exactly what I had to do. To get back at them would take careful planning. To get out, I had to go back in."

Bishop climbed out of a cab in front of an old, dilapidated townhouse on Avenue D in NYC. He reluctantly rang an unmarked buzzer.

Diego Phoenix, a grizzled old queen with a thick, black toupee, leaned out of a second-story window. "Oh, god help us," he said in the hoarse whisper of a lifetime smoker. He tossed Bishop a key attached to a parachute.

Diego met Bishop at the door leaning heavily on a cane, his nearly toothless mouth stained red from wine, his cigar never leaving his fingers. "Look what the hellcat dragged in."

"Hello, old friend. How's it been?"

The small, dark apartment was covered in paintings of faraway galaxies, strewn about art supplies, and long ignored filth. "Well, I figured out how to work the Lottery, just enough to survive undetected." He struggled through a Sammy Davis Jr. number, his attempt at tap dancing resulting in a harsh coughing fit.

Bishop wasted no time. "Diego, you know why I've come."

"Don't I?" he said after the coughing had abated.

"You were the very core of the Starseed program. You developed the protocols. They sent me because the program is being reinstated and your brand of expertise is needed. I know what you're going to say. But this time will be different. We'll train them for good, using your rulebook." He struggled to say the next part. "It's your national duty to this country."

"Oh, horseshit. That worked the first time but not anymore. Save your breath. BD left me on that target for three days. That troglodyte knew damn well I was in danger. He's my nemesis, you know," he says with an arch of an eyebrow. "I fulfilled my duty because I got paid for it. Well, a little bit anyway. Besides, I couldn't do it now if I tried. They threw me away after I was broken. You can tell those jackals they can eat my ass."

"They're not giving us a choice, Diego. There's something bigger going here and people are being killed for it." His words resurrected the pain of seeing those photographs. His team were good people, dedicated. "We can use this opportunity to bring the whole thing down using your method. We have to be close to the machinery to throw ourselves upon the gears."

"Are we activists now? Is that it?" Diego sat down heavily, emptying his glass of wine. "I knew I shouldn't have opened the damned door."

Back at the Nest, Bishop pauses the story to remove his shoes, as is his custom upon entering his sanctuary: a dimly lit, cathedral-sized cavern adjacent to the base. A path leads to a large greenhouse that contains small trees and a collection of exotic birds free to roam within. The sound of a man-made waterfall can be heard in the distance, along with the soft cooing of the birds.

Bishop takes a deep, centering breath and turns around to face Del and Mills, Valentina and Bodhi behind them. "Tina, why don't you show Bodhi the Cockatoos. They've missed you." Bishop winks.

Valentina takes the cue and leads her grandson by the hand out of earshot.

He turns and gives Del a long, hard look. "I know it stings, but you're smart enough to realize this was the only way we could play it. This thing is bigger than all of us and I'm sorry I had to lie to you." He looks at Mills, then back to Del. "Would you like to know why I sent you on a goose chase through the desert to bring this guy back to life?"

Sterile fluorescent lighting flooded the black-boards and grade-school desks and chairs. Aside from the occasional throat clearing, the room was silent, as soldiers of different branches were being given an advanced placement test.

Mills sat studying the question on the paper in front of him, his hair buzzed short and his skin devoid of tattoos. *It's your birthday. Someone gives you a calfskin wallet. How do you react? a) I would appreciate it. b) Thank them for the wallet. c) I wouldn't accept it.*

Mills sensed something was off. He looked around the room and noticed flickering of the fluorescent lighting on the back wall. Inside that flickering, he saw impressions being projected against the wall, shadows of words that were once there. One word at a time. The more he looked, the more he realized there was a synchronized rhythm to the projections. He closed his eyes, counted, then opened his eyes to catch the words as they appeared emblazoned on the back wall. *One two three. Open.* It reminded him of those pictures that don't appear to harbor anything at face

56

value, but in fact, contain hidden images the mind can access when looking beyond the picture itself. *One two three. Open.* FIND. THE. RED. STAG. He looked around the room and realized he was the only one seeing it.

He got up and scanned the room. He saw nothing resembling a horse anywhere. He headed for the door and followed the long hallway beyond it with its series of closed and unmarked doors. No one stopped him. He continued down the maze of hallways until he arrived at the office of Lt. Col. Joseph Bishop. A small, red stag insignia was placed next to Bishop's title on the door.

He entered and a young, flat-topped Leland looked up from his desk, peering over thick, black-rimmed glasses. "Staff Sergeant Mills. He's been expecting you," he said, pointing to another door for Mills to enter.

Bishop looked up from a bank of ten monitors, all showing the many test rooms in progress. "You know, the experts say that statistically, this level of perception is available to only one out of a thousand people. Would you like to see where it can take you?"

At an undisclosed base in Maryland, a room full of recruits were seated in a small auditorium, a podium and several flags on stands occupying the elevated platform stage. Bishop entered and took a position behind the podium, clearing his throat. "In a recent interview, ex-president Jimmy Carter revealed a truth we thought would never see the light of day. A Soviet plane went down in the air and spy satellites failed to locate the wreckage. Intelligence Director at the time, Admiral Stansfield Turner, consulted remote viewers who found the plane and agents on the ground were dispatched to the location, resulting in a successful recovery mission. Gentlemen, the creator of the Starseed program, and the father of Remote Viewing, my dear friend, the legendary Diego Phoenix."

A young recruit whispered over the polite applause, "The guy who wrote our book? He's still alive?"

Diego struggled to the podium. "Thank you for that warm introduction. There have been times when I didn't receive as much. This is a field where reputations are more easily ruined than celebrated," he rasped as a brush fire would. "You boys should already know who I am. My pretty face is on the back of those books you all got." He framed his nearly toothless grin with his hands. "Mystics for years have taught us that we are hindered by the world only because we are told to believe that we are defined by the physical senses based on conscious awareness. Mystics are more likely to access and expand on information collected through the subconscious, as it tends to not be limited to only that which can be experienced and explained through the physical senses. They taught the world of light, pure unentangled thoughts and feelings. Have any of you ever experienced a state like that? Show of hands."

A few in the audience sheepishly held their hands slightly above their heads.

"How many haven't experienced it?"

Even fewer hands popped up.

"Half of you aren't raising your hands at all."

A few embarrassed laughs followed.

"Have I confused you yet?" He paused, his breath labored. "Remote Viewing is indicative of another dimension that transcends physical matter, energy, space, and time. The sixth sense and the powers associated with it are completely ignored by our current educational system. Together, we will remove any doubts you may have developed since childhood and discover the full potential of your mind. I'm not here to teach you anything. I'm here to unteach you."

In preparation for their operational tasks in psychic spy missions, the men were given lessons in the history, protocol, and practice of Remote Viewing, with detailed definitions and guides. They were shown films on military information support operations and situational awareness. A Peruvian shaman guided them through meditation to release negative energy, using advanced techniques to alleviate distractions and prepare them for entering an altered state of consciousness, while remaining present to the flow of information received from outside the senses.

After rigorous psychological testing, Diego began training the thirty men that made the first cut, his gentle guidance second nature to him. "First stage: ideograms. Keep the consciousness busy, allowing the subconscious free to explore. Second stage: physical contact with the site. Imagine seeing colors as in a dream. What does it smell like there? The further in you go in, the physical connection becomes stronger until you can see what's there with deeper clarity and precision."

With practice came ritual. The men adopted behaviors to assist the start of each session. A young recruit put on his lucky hat. Another, a good looking buck named Hooch, did fingertip pushups. Mills blared heavy metal music through headphones.

Diego presented a locked briefcase with an image inside. He wrote down target coordinates on a whiteboard. The class began drawing their ideograms until time was up and they had to present their work. Most of the drawings were indecipherable. Mills had drawn a circle inside a circle inside another circle.

The case was unlocked and the contents removed. A bull's eye. Mills's image was a finely detailed match. "Hot damn!" Diego said. The other men applauded.

Blackwell stopped in to view the progress from the back of the room. He seemed ever so pleased.

The class had been reduced to six men. Diego

scribbles the words "Remote Influencing" on a clear piece of plastic that was simultaneously illuminated on an overhead projector behind him. He wrote as he spoke. "Stage 6. Now we enter into the subconscious of a targeted individual. It's like interviewing the subconscious mind but the subconscious mind speaks a different language. The conscious and the subconscious talk to each other through an interpreter. Remote Influencing is a physical discipline, a mental martial art, and the body is the interpreter. You must train your body to respond to the subliminal transfer of recollections, anxieties, and desires to conscious accessible thought. Impressions constitute memories and fears, as well as analysis. You want to send something to the target that the subconscious mind can convey to the body. The subconscious mind does not effectively respond to direct commands, but how they are made to feel. Are any of you asleep yet?"

Hooch coughed. "Is he allowed to smoke in here?" he whispered to Mills.

"The first failsafe is to have a handler with you at all times. Under the Foreign Intelligence Surveillance Act, you are protected by the use of mandatory two-person control. It is vital you never try it without a handler. Number two, get out quickly. When you say 'session end', be ready. Which leads to three, detox or die. You must detox after each session in which you access another person and detox takes twice the length of your session. You can get sucked into the other person's emotions, moralities, moods and out-look in life. Anything in that person's mind becomes embedded in yours. You will ask yourself, is that my target's feelings or my feelings? When you start de-toxing, the answer is yes to both. When you access someone, you will be exposed to feelings you're not accustomed to. You will need to ask yourself, is that what I normally feel? Depending on who your target is, you may experience what it feels like to be fine with molesting children. You've got to follow the impres-sions to work your way back. Staying too long can be extremely dangerous. You run the risk of never coming back. Number four, never Remote Influence military personnel unless instructed by your superior or face criminal charges punishable by time in Leav-enworth."

The class was paired off with individual handlers, technicians in white coats there to guide the men as they laid back in reclining chairs hooked up to heart monitors. Diego activated a metronome at the front of the class and walked through the room. "Use your breathing to go deep inside and let yourself open up. If the word is car, the subconscious lets you feel that new car smell, feel the wind on the face. You first tim-ers need to rely on your ideograms until the body gets used to it and begins communicating with the subcon-scious."

All of the men quickly grew frustrated, all except for Mills, who held a concentrated yet peaceful look on his face. He sleep-talked through his mission as Leland, his handler, diligently wrote down the relayed Intel. Mills was a standout natural. Diego took notice.

The next day, Diego wheeled in a TV and invited Mills and Leland to join him at the front of the room. "It's imperative that you create a scenario whereby the targeted individual's subconscious needs to be distracted and disarmed. This is achieved by probing the subject's psyche and creating a nebulous scene whereby they are enticed into cooperation. Know your target. Utilize their belief system and motivations as a guide."

He turned on the TV to reveal live security footage of a guard sitting at a small desk, working his post at the perimeter of the base. "The object is to get this security guard to remove his shirt."

A few students snickered.

"What, it's my class!" Diego smiled mischievously. "Remember, don't tell him what to do. Make him think he thought of it himself. You're communicating directly to his subconscious. Figure out who he wants to invite in." He initiated the metronome.

After Leland prepared the session, Mills closed his eyes and began.

Tom Brady of the New England Patriots drives up to the gate in a bright red Jeep Wrangler. He smiles brightly as he addresses the security guard. "Hey, we're at a training camp not too far from here. Everybody's pooping out today and I want to run a few more drills.

Wanna throw a few rounds with me? You look like you used to play a little ball."

The security guard is over the moon! His hero, the GOAT! He doesn't hesitate and leaves his post to join the quarterback on the patch of yard in the front of the building. They throw the ball for what feels like an eternity. Brady doesn't break a sweat, but the guard is beginning to perspire profusely. He still has hours before his shift is over and decides he must remove his shirt before it gets too unwearable. He takes it off.

The class watched the live feed of the guard sitting at his desk, trying to read a newspaper. He shifted in his chair in apparent discomfort. He rubbed the back of his neck as he flipped the pages of the paper aimlessly. Finally, he stood up, unbuttoned his army green fatigue, tossed it aside, and sat back down in his starched white tee-shirt.

Tom Brady catches the last vault and holds it, walking towards the guard. "Ah man, I have to get going. What's your name?"

"I'm Jeff."

"Thanks, Jeff. And if we win tomorrow, I'll know it's because of you." Tom makes the shape of a heart with his hands and places it over his own heart.

"The objective has been achieved. What did you use?" Diego asked.

Mills was coming back from the session, rubbing his eyes. "An opportunity he couldn't refuse."

"Thank you, John. An effective approach. Always leave them wanting more."

It was late in the day and Mills was perusing the vending machine near the mess hall. Diego loomed in the shadows, illuminated by the pull of his cigar. "You looking for something with a little more kick?"

Mills hesitated. "I'm good."

"Come on. It's the holidays. Never know if this Christmas will be your last."

Mills followed Diego to his quarters and once inside, Diego handed him a cup of brandy, refilling his own. "You remind me of me, John. I was always a bit psychic and when this program came along, I was like a fish to water. They brought us in to Remote Influence the top levels of the Politburo. Their finance minister was suspected of colluding with banks behind the Order. It was tense, so I stayed with them for what was an awfully long time and apparently attracted the attention of the Soviet version of ourselves. We already knew we were competing with them. Their advanced programs were up and running long before we were. They were way ahead of us and had learned some nasty tricks.

"It was too late before I realized they weren't there to observe. They were there to take me out. I felt like I was attacked by an immense ice shadow, strangling, drowning and mauling me. I couldn't get away. It held me, burning me with ice. Somehow I dragged myself out, but after detox, the lights just wouldn't come on anymore. Whole corridors of my brain were locked down and sealed with darkness." Diego took a long pull of his brandy and stared at the floor. "You see, the thing about our art is that it isn't indefensible. Even to us."

"Do you know who did this to you?"

"I have some idea. I tried to heal myself but it wouldn't budge. It's too heavy."

"Mind if I take a look in there?"

"This old thing?" Diego smirked.

It's mid-morning in a lush forest. Diego is standing at an easel in a clearing by a waterfall, wearing a yellow ascot, cheeks flush with a healthy glow. Mills approaches from behind and studies the image on the canvas, an intricate painting of the Cosmos. "I didn't know you could paint."

"It passes the time."

A loud snore interrupts them. "What is that?" Mills asks, searching for the sound's origin.

Diego recoils. "Whatever you do, don't wake him up!"

Mills follows the direction of the sound, behind the waterfall, to an overgrown opening of a den. In stark contrast to the glorious day, the light is dim with a temperature so cold Mills can see his breath. A few feet from the opening of the cavity, a huge bear, black as night, is splayed out in its torpor. Mills turns to Diego, who is standing close behind him, shivering from fright. "What do you see?"

Diego is terrified. He whispers, "I see what you see. A giant bear that will tear us to shreds if we wake it up!"

Mills produces a small bouquet of blue irises and hands them to Diego, who's mood brightens at the sight of them. "Maybe the bear would appreciate this beautiful day," he says and begins to remove debris covering the entrance.

Diego is tense and protests. "But what if the bear wakes up hungry and attacks?"

"You just have to show him the way out. Nice and gentle."

Diego reluctantly helps him with one hand, clutching the irises to his chest in the other. As they clear the entrance, the flood of sunlight causes the bear to stir.

Mills soothes with his voice. "Hold your hand up and slowly back out. Don't make direct eye contact, but keep a close look at the bear as you back away."

The bear shakes the slumber out of his matted fur head and takes a step towards them. "Hey, fella. Hey. How ya doin'? Now, don't get too close. You be a good boy. I know this is confusing for you. I know this is your home. We understand. We're not going to take your bed." Diego says as they take slow, measured steps backwards, passing the waterfall, the bear matching their every step. The day wraps them in warmth. The bear finds a path to the river to fetch his breakfast. Diego beams at Mills. The vibrant color of the forest illuminates around them.

Diego snapped back to attention in his ashy quarters, visibly better. "My dear boy! You've rectified me," he cried, throwing his arms around Mills. "I knew you were especially gifted, son, but I never thought I could be saved. Thank you, dear boy. Thank you!"

"Nothing you didn't already have in you," he

said, shy to receive praise.

The next day, recruits were startled by the curious tapping sounds heard echoing the hollowed hallway. Diego was dancing his way to class, sans cane, singing, "Who can take a sunrise, sprinkle it with dew."

The men were finishing up in the locker room, their spirits soaring before leaving for Christmas break. Hooch was giving Mills a hard time about not coming out with them. "Lulu's cousin is coming in from Flagstaff for liberty. We're all going to get drunk and try not to suck at bowling."

"Thanks, I'll pass," Mills said.

"You know her cousin's a girl, right?" He continued to rib him but shut it down as Bishop approached.

"John, I'm going to need you to drop off today's report summary."

"I already gave it to my handler."

"There's a protocol issue. I need to speak with you in private. Come by my quarters at twenty hundred." Bishop's tone is stern.

After he left the room and out of earshot, Hooch and the others made "Oooh" sounds.

Mills made his way on foot, head hanging low. The holidays had become a time of strain for him. After the death of his adoptive mother years ago, he became estranged from the abusive father he no longer felt he owed anything to. He managed his feelings of loss by shutting down those very feelings when they came up. He had no use for them.

A group of soldiers approached, walking in the opposite direction. After they had passed, one soldier called out, "Look, boys! It's a ghost! Boo!" Mills continued walking, paying them no mind.

He climbed the porch of the white, two-story house warmly lit from the inside and knocked on the door, his report summary under his arm. Bishop's voice could be heard from inside. "Would you get that, Darling?"

Del answered the door in a thin tee-shirt and a surprised look on her face. Mills met her eyes briefly, then lowered his head. "Uh, I'm here to see Colonel Bishop."

"Dad, delivery boy!" Her voice was playfully sing-song. She sauntered off, leaving the door open for Mills to enter.

Bishop greeted him in the foyer, a glass of wine in hand. "The summary you asked for, sir," he said, handing Bishop the paperwork.

Bishop traded him for the glass of wine. "Hope you're hungry, John."

The table was set for four. Del helped her mother serve up an exquisite Christmas dinner as Bishop delighted in extolling stories steeped in Del's rebellious youth. Bishop and Valentina bathed in each other's presence and retired early.

Del grabbed a bottle of wine and suggested they

sit closer to the fire. "So, what passes for fun out here? Army bases have always been so boring to me."

"Oh, just your average, run-of-the-mill top-secret compound. Not a whole lot that's entertaining. We get a lot of stars out here, though. Want to take a look?"

"How about a social lubricant?" Del retrieved two small pills wrapped in foil from the front pocket of her tight jeans.

"What's that you got there?"

"Just your average, run-of-the-mill, top-shelf ecstasy. Always entertaining. Race ya!" She handed him a pill and popped her own.

He took a moment to consider the ramifications. The presence of this beautiful woman wiped his mind and he swallowed the pill.

They stepped outside to walk the grounds of a nearly empty base. Del spotted a small park with a wooden play structure. She bolted for the swing set. Mills took the position behind her, pushing her on a swing with a squeak that reverberated throughout the dark night.

"What do you do for my father exactly?"

"I'm not supposed to talk about it. Even with the boss's daughter."

"The plot thickens."

"It sounds exciting but it's not. In order for it to be effective, intelligence work has to be done behind the scenes and out of the spotlight. Some people choose to ridicule what we're doing out of ignorance, or maybe fear, when in fact it takes serious concentration and vulnerability to achieve success at it. Not easy. But I get it. That we are able to do what we do is hard for most people to accept."

She jumped off the swing and kissed him, taking his hand and leading him to a little ladder connected to the lookout deck attached to the jungle gym fort. The drug was taking effect and their bodies followed. He went hard and fast, never losing contact with her doe-eyed gaze. She clutched him, tearing at his fatigues, hooking her legs around his. The night sky was the backdrop to his handsome face. His expression held the intensity of one attempting to solve a complex equation. It felt as if he knew what she was thinking as she was thinking it. All the other guys were wham bam without a thank you, ma'am. John was his own creature. She had always hated that feeling of falling. It made her dizzy. There was nothing she could do to help herself because, at this moment, he was everything.

Dawn was breaking as Del snuck back into her father's house, trying her best not to disturb the crisp morning peace. Bishop, already awake at the dining room table, looked up briefly from his files. "Shirt's on backwards," he teased.

Mills and Leland sat calmly at a metal table in an observation room at the lab. They had responded to a call for an important session and were ready to launch over an hour ago. As they sat, Mills was being observed from behind a one-way mirror. In the darkened room beyond the glass, Diego and Bishop were joined by Blackwell, wearing an impeccable tux, and a wealthy Senator from South Carolina, late to arrive.

"I believe him to be the greatest natural Remote Influencer of our time," Diego offered, directing his comment at their guest. He was told funding was on the line and was trying to be on his best behavior.

Bishop turned on a small TV monitor on the control panel in front of them. "In order for this to work, the target must be live," he said, offering the Senator the remote control. "Would you like to do the honors?"

Intrigued, the Senator took the remote and flipped to C-SPAN, where a House Judiciary Committee Oversight Hearing was underway. "I can pick anyone?"

"Whomever you like."

"Oh, this should be fun.

The Deputy Attorney General seemed to know and then not know answers to questions pertaining to ongoing investigations over unfair bias due to excessive campaign contributions. The Chair recognized the gentlewoman Committee member next to speak.

"Her. That old battle-axe in the red dress. I quite like her. She's feisty."

As she moved on her questions, she began briefly reviewing investigations by several alphabet agents that led to the arrests of many homegrown terrorists.

"What would you like her to do?" Diego mused.

The Senator replied, "I've always imagined she'd be a good dancer." His glee was difficult to hide.

Bishop informed Mills through an intercom, "We've got a target." Leland checked the heart monitors and gave Bishop a nod through the mirrored glass.

Diego leaned into the mic. "It's time to get down and boogie!" he said, doing his best Saturday Night Fever moves.

Mills closed his eyes. They watched the live feed in anticipation. Within minutes, the gentlewoman stopped her line of questioning, stood up and started shaking her hips. This created an obvious disturbance and the Chair called the Committee to order. The speaker lost her train of thought and ultimately excused himself.

The Senator was impressed. "That's the most amazing thing I've ever seen"

"I assure you, this is the tip of the iceberg," Blackwell says. "This weapons system is the single most dominant and lethal project we've ever launched. It simply has no limitations. We have stages planned that would make this the most valuable asset we've ever had in the field. Capable of anything."

"We're still testing the limits, B.D. Of the human being. Of his psyche. There's only one John Mills."

Diego's response was undermining, but he didn't care. He had to protect his star pupil.

Blackwell was quick to correct himself. "I'll admit. I know nothing of the fundamentals of how this is done. That's for the experts. Right?" He put a heavy paw on Diego's shoulders, making him feel the weight.

"To be clear, we're talking about a realm we don't fully understand. If you recall, B.D., it's been abused in the past, with dire consequences. It absolutely has limitations. You want to play big dick with someone else's mind, know what the fuck you're talking about."

Blackwell contained the storm brewing in his belly. "My esteemed colleague, Mr. Phoenix, has a point. We're still testing the limitations of these incredible assets. All in all, I think everyone here can agree that this program needs to continue to develop and at triple last year's budget. And of course, we need to stay black. Bishop, would you be so kind as to accompany the Senator back to the airport? You can bring him up to speed on the ways and means of the budgetary guidelines."

"Of course." Bishop notified Leland he would return shortly and walked the Senator out.

Not quite back to consciousness, Mills sensed a disturbance and searched for Diego. He found him in his office, alone with Blackwell. The two men were arguing.

"You've got a big mouth, even for a flamboyant

faggot."

Diego cooly responded, "You know the fundamental difference between you and me? It's not talent or vision or ambition. It's character. Your lack of imagination is crippling. You and your kind don't understand the way the universe works because you built yourself up so high that most of the negative shit you've done won't catch you for a long time. But those of us with a higher purpose know that it's your shadow on the wall. And that for every action, there is an equal and opposite reaction. So, come in here and do what you're going to do, little man. Makes no difference to me."

Blackwell, filled with hot fury, lunged at Diego, stabbing him in the neck with a double-edged, spear point blade. "Fucking insect," he spat and walked out, wiping his hand on a handkerchief. He placed a call and told the person on the other end of the line, "Got a mess in the little faggot's office. Clean it up. I'm off to Der Vorstand." He headed towards his chopper without a glance back.

Mills came back into his mind, ripping his monitors off and struggling to stand. His legs collapsed underneath him. Leland picked him up from the ground and returned him to his chair. "Slow down, Milly. You're detoxing. Do the breathing."

"They got Diego," he gasped.

"Diego's fine, man. You're just getting blowback. You gotta relax."

"No. Gotta go." Mills grappled for the door.

Leland reluctantly helped him by buoying his weight onto one shoulder. When they got to Diego's office, they saw Diego on the floor, holding his blood-soaked scarf-covered throat, reaching for his cigar. Leland dropped Mills off on a nearby chair to attend to Diego, attempting to staunch the blood flow as Mills looked on helplessly. He was still too weak to support his own weight, so he dropped to his knees and crawled over to his beloved mentor. When he reached him, he put his face up close next to his. "What did he do to you? Why?" Mills couldn't stop the tears.

Through the last plume of cigar smoke, Diego regarded his protégé with pride. "We're not done, son. Not by a long shot. I won't be too hard to find." His eyes lost their light and he was gone.

Mills was emotionally unmoored. "I'm going back in."

"Milly, you're a mess! You can't stack without detoxing. You're going to be fucking mush. Remember the training. You want to come back, right?"

"I'm going to burn that motherfucker." His tone could cut steel. He hoisted himself up and returned to the lab, Leland at his heels. Leaving him no choice, Leland hooked him up to the heart monitor. "Your vitals are all over the place, man!"

Mills reached forward and started the metronome with the swipe of a finger. He went under quickly, his consciousness rising up and out of his body.

With razor-sharp precision, he spotted his target.

3. DER VORSTAND

The black helicopter cleared the darkening mountains as lights of an illustrious mansion shimmered in the distance. It set down on a helipad adjacent to an airfield boasting innumerable private jets.

Ushered by a tuxedoed concierge, Blackwell passed by a long line of luxury vehicles with names like Rolls-Royce, Maybach and Bentley. As he neared the main house, he took the customary leave of his security detail and entered through the grand foyer.

Guests were led into an enormous ballroom with ornate ceilings, antique marble and detailed tile work throughout. Frescoes and fine art hung from walls, with classic fountains adding to the grandiose landscape. The room offered casino-style games, as impeccably dressed guests played high-stakes roulette and craps while a spiffy looking Lyle Lovett sang Exit Music by Radiohead alongside an extensive orchestra. The center of the room held a large, glass case containing an interactive virtual reality model of an opulent ship dubbed the SS Canaan. Lucent Dossier performed dramatic acrobatic air shows on silk high above the heads of the guests.

Blackwell made his way to the kitchen, taking a moment to chastise the celebrity chef in the throes of prep chaos, as the staff prepared exotic delicacies and extravagant showpieces. Blackwell stuck his fingers into a bowl of foie gras terrine and stuffed them into his mouth, twice, sullying the food in the bowl. The chef and staff nervously laughed it off, knowing full well who he was, their spines tightening by his presence. He ate his fill and walked out. Once gone, the room could breathe again.

Blackwell moved through the main ballroom like a shark. He was all business. An ex-President approached him, arms outstretched. "Well, they'll just let anyone in here. Whaddya say B.D.?"

Blackwell scoffed. "Apparently so." He ignored the gesture and headed straight for the nearest bar. "Scotch. Double," he growled.

Amschel Rotterdam, his cup of wealth runneth over, edged over to Blackwell, his head hung unnaturally low for his thin, wiry frame. Speaking in a British accent with a voice and cadence reflecting years of paramount privilege, he said, "Your face is looking particularly craggy today." He pointed to the blood on Blackwell's sleeve. "Busy afternoon?"

"Quite."

"Glad to see you're deeply committed." He looked around the grand ballroom. "Have you spoken to Jean Pierre from Credit de Swiss?"

"He's here. I saw him on the way in."

"Yes, indeed." Amschel moved in closer to Blackwell's face, lowering his altogether dreary register to a crawl. "Make sure it's clear. It's a billion per seat. We're accepting US dollars or gold. No exceptions. I don't care what the Chinks have to say about it." He straightened, seeing the President of Nigeria dressed in traditional robes. "Well, it looks as though someone came ready for bed."

In a secluded area of the party, Amschel spoke privately with a small group of men. "And then they'll pay us for the vaccine that's going to bloody sterilize them!" The group laughed haughtily.

Evelyn Rockford, a well-dressed fop of short stature and enormous wealth, spoke in a lilting Southern drawl. "Well, how much for the vaccine?"

"When all is said and done, a thousand dollars per shot."

"Poor things! They'll have to take out a personal loan!" The group erupted with laughter.

A bookish, paunchy man with a milky pallor from worry wanders aimlessly over to where Blackwell is speaking with a Russian Oligarch.

"Digby Lange! You fabulous nerd. Tell our friend here what you're working on."

Digby, feeling out of place by matter of course, spoke quickly. "It's basically utilizing a network of microwave transmitters throughout the grid to manipulate certain frequencies in the cortex and influence perception."

"Blah blah blah science. What my loquacious little Oppenheimer is saying is, basically, he's invented electronic crowd control."

"Well, it's significantly more complex than that.

It has the capacity to increasingly subdue the masses, weaken targeted individuals, and if need be, blanket entire communities."

Blackwell patted him on the back. "Good stuff, Digs. Do let us know when you fire that thing up, will you?"

The cacophonous bellow of an animal horn signaled the men to take leave of their casino games and make their way towards a back amber chamber of mahogany walls, pictures of grand estates in gold frames, and the smell of cigar smoke permanently permeating the air.

Blackwell, drink in hand, spotted an old friend. "Geronimo, you old bastard. You've never looked better."

A tall Saudi Arabian National, clean shaven, short haired, and wearing a tailored suit, said, "Two new kidneys!" He flashed two thumbs up.

The lights began lowering in the chamber and a promotional video was cast from an overhead projector in the ceiling on the only bare wall in the room. A narrated tour of the SS Canaan informed the guests of what their membership will buy. "Design your own ten-thousand square feet lavish suite with all the amenities. Twenty-four-hour concierge service. Access to next level medicine. Wounds that heal instantly via stem cells." A montage showcased the SS Canaan's luxury pools, sweeping staircases, and impeccable accommodations. Images of the boat's movie theatre and planetarium above plush recliners, extensive library, elaborate restaurants, prestigious art galleries, and a church with a cathedral ceiling.

The presentation concluded and guests were invited to explore the mansion's decadent grounds. Roman baths with large jacuzzis were occupied by fat businessmen getting scrubbed down by naked young men and women. Calico covered cabanas provided privacy for crude bodily pleasures with tragically young girls herded by a tall, dark, and very handsome man by the name of Christopher Blackwell. B.D.'s only son fully enjoyed the fruits of his father's labor for the highest echelon of society and because of it, woefully lacked any moral compass. The privilege made him a creature more loathsome than pestilence.

When he spied his father ambling over, Christopher escorted his father to the cabana awaiting him to show off a new girl wearing a doll's dress. "Iceland," he said. "We picked her up from a museum lagging behind on a school field trip. I think you're going to like her."

Blackwell examined the girl thoroughly. He checked her teeth, the roots of her blonde hair, and turned her over, lifting her skirt to inspect her undercarriage. "Are you sure she's a virgin? One can never be sure."

"Only one way to find out." Christopher flashed a smile reminiscent of the Cheshire Cat if it had ever mated with a snake. He slithered off and resumed his position in his own cabana. A constituent in the Lolita Express was there waiting for him and refilled their goblets upon his return. As Christopher nonchalantly continued the story he was telling about the stacks of dead bodies he saw while living in Manila, he summoned over the young girl who was shivering on the far end of his cabana. She was gaunt and sickly and he chose her for himself because her sad eyes excited him. He began fingering her under the impossibly short dress he made all the girls wear, the sedatives he plied her with making her docile and unquestioning.

Blackwell chased the young blonde girl around, removing the articles of his tux as he did, his saggy flesh airing out. He unhooked a leash and collar hanging from a hook on the wall of his cabana, and slowly approached her. She was backed into a corner and had nowhere to run. He gently slid the collar around her neck and pulled hard on the leash.

Blackwell sits at a massive oak table wearing a crown and velvet robes of red and gold, his lauding court seated beneath him. The table is overflowing with food, an apple-mouthed pig on a gilded platter placed within reach. He stuffs his face using both hands, his chest heaving as he piles the food into his mouth, his hungry subjects looking on.

Suddenly, he hears roaring laughter. He looks down and sees that he is not wearing pants. His subjects point and laugh at his tiny, button-like penis. He grows furious and scans the crowd, his eyes landing on two shadowy figures standing in the back of the room. Mills and

84

the ghostly visage of Diego Phoenix, bloody ascot intact, glare at him with utter disdain and contempt.

He jumps to his feet in a rage. "Seize them!" he screams, pointing in their direction, but they are gone. The laughter swells to riotous levels.

He snapped back to the cabana and looked down at the sobbing little girl beneath him, his flaccid penis a mere skin tag between his legs. Through gritted teeth, he growled, "Mills."

Returning to his body, Mills was red hot and imbued with Blackwell's rage. He ripped off the heart monitor and grabbed Leland by the throat. "You're a dead man!"

"Protocols, Milly! You've got to get him out of you!" Leland did his best to restrain him.

Bishop, home from accompanying the Senator the airport, was reading in his study when the angry call came in. "Lockdown. Nobody in or out," Blackwell spat over the loud chopping noise of the helo.

"What's happened?"

"I own this base. I own you and everything in it. You'll do what the fuck I say!" He hung up in Bishop's ear.

Bishop quickly returned to the lab to find Mills in the throes of a gruesome detox. Leland quickly briefed him and his alarm grew. "John, he's coming for you."

Leland jumped into action. "He won't want him if he's dead. Help me. We have to bring his temperature down. We'll perfuse him with adenosine and lignocaine. The injections will put his heart in a state of suspended animation. But we won't have much time."

"Well, if we don't try, he'll kill him anyway. Let's make this happen." Bishop began assisting Leland in the procedure to stop John's heart.

Blackwell deboarded his chopper and stormed the lab with his security detail, fuming. "Where the fuck is he?"

Bishop and Leland were busy performing CPR on Mills, the dull tone from the heart monitor indicated he was flatlining on the gurney. When Blackwell entered the lab, Bishop ceased administering compressions, signaling to Leland to stop delivering rescue breaths. "He didn't make it back. He went into asystole twenty minutes ago. We've tried everything."

"We'll see how dead he is," Blackwell said, grabbing a gun from the shoulder holster of his guard and pointing it at John's lifeless body.

Leland quickly jumped in between Mills and the gun with his hands up. "We can study him. Find out what happened along the way. But we can't do that if you put holes in him."

Bishop tried another approach. "He went off the reservation. We have no idea what transpired while he was under, what he saw. All we know is we just lost our best asset."

Blackwell lowered the gun, his rage still festering. "Train someone to pick up the slack."

"You don't understand. He was in a class of his own. He was so advanced, Diego could no longer teach him. And with Diego gone, John Mills was the program."

Blackwell handed the gun back to his guard, disgusted. "Well, fuck me. We just shit the bed." He wiped his brow with his tuxedo kerchief. "Shut it down. Shut the whole goddamn thing down!"

4. SPOILED SOVEREIGNTY

A black Concord Private Jet lands in Paris Le Bourget Airport. A cavalcade of security, black town cars, and a white Rolls-Royce Phantom await the arrival of the Rotterdam Clan disembarking the aircraft. Amschel Rotterdam, his white-blonde, painfully fit wife Vanessa Rotterdam, wearing large, black sunglasses, the elder children Annesley and Laughton, and ten-year-old Winnie, white-blonde hair like her mother, are ushered into the Phantom and the caravan drives off.

The Paris Police Prefecture have closed off the two-kilometer-wide line of Avenue des Champs Elysees that connects the Place de la Concorde and Etoile Square with its famous Arc de Triomphe, known for it's most expensive and world-famous shopping. The confusion causes panic and a group of boys being redirected by Police blocking the road ask in French if it is, in fact, a bomb scare and should they be worried. "Circulez, il n'y a rien à voir!" The officer tells the boys to move along.

The rows of exclusive stores are now barren, save for the Rotterdam Clan, ready to shop. "Just like Goering," Amschel mumbles to no one in particular.

"I'll take four of those and three of these," Annesley says, entirely in her element. The family point their fingers at their desired objects as they walk through the empty stores with an eager staff at their heels, packaging up their requests as soon as they are spouted. As elitist, germaphobic hypochondriacs, there is very little interaction between the Rotterdams and the help. Instead, they berate the merchandise for their own amusement. "Ugh! Italian designers. Fucking animals," Laughton says with a flick of his fingers.

They lunch at Alain Ducasse au Plaza Athénée. The all-white interior drips with crystal chandeliers, the tables are solid oak, and the chairs are made of soft leather. An expertly coordinated ballet is performed around them, one serveur per family member, placing down the multitude of courses in unison. The maitre d' acts as the conductor, describing the fine points of the food and wine, pared course by course. "As you might already know, our chef earned three Michelin stars for his unparalleled vision and culinary genius!" He beams with pride, waiting for approval that never comes.

The Rotterdams aren't impressed by anything, not bothering to hide their incessant eye-rolling. They are displeased by everything set before them. The chef's meticulous care in creating plates of food comparable to avant-garde art is lost on them. "Yuck. Make this go away!" They ignore the food completely and instead take pills from gilded cases.

Annesley is on her phone at the table watching Frankie Q on Topp App, who is dressed in a traditional Geisha costume and makeup, including a pencilled in moustache. Old-timey cartoon music and sound effects accompany today's show. Frankie Q pretends to be surprised by the doorbell ringing. A large, brown box is delivered and when he opens it, a tiny person pops out, covered in packing foam. "Yay! My old one was broken." His previous assistant, also a tiny person, is sprawled out in a garbage can with x's over his eyes.

Laughton looks over Annesley's shoulder, cracking up. She shoves his head and says, "Get your own!"

A serveur comes over to remove Laughton's untouched plate. He grabs a lobster fork and pokes him, causing pinpricks of blood to surface. "Bad dog!" he says, cracking himself up.

Amschel and Vanessa sit together on the other side of the table, stone-faced. Vanessa smokes from a gold-plated vape pen. "You used to like me in Paris," Vanessa sighs.

"I used to like myself," he replies flatly.

They return home to their estate, Doden Hall, located in Montecito, California, their Concord Private Jet landing on an airstrip connected to the property. Opulence manifest, the palatial exterior is made of rocks hand-picked and sourced from five different quarries, creating an appearance that is both monumental and dramatically ethereal.

The vast interior is adorned with decorative beams of patterned marble throughout, the rooms dimly lit as expensive perfume counters would be, the huge rooms minimally designed with the very best of everything. A personal Odeon is an elevator ride away and two swimming pools are located off third-floor balconies, one for each of the older children. A pair of extinct giraffes are housed just outside the balcony of the youngest daughter's bedroom. Panic rooms spread throughout the house are both stylish and military grade. The full-time staff has living quarters located below the media room. The twenty-five thousand square foot, two-floor garage boasts a machine shop, living room, office, library, and luxury kitchen. Countless cars rest atop white stainless steel counters under bright halogen lamps, untouched. Throughout the gilded estate, Amschel's remarkable art collection, objects of 15th century theatre, demands a degree of calm, setting the stage for entertaining elite with their circling wreathes of cigar smoke.

Amschel is a treatise on what it is like to be so wealthy and powerful that there is nothing else to want for, his materialism deeply unfulfilling. Because complete control does not exist, he tries to control his surroundings. Nothing is ever up to par. Excellence is the only thing he'll accept, a demand that knows no limits. First class or no class is his motto. When an ostentatious statue of a gorilla was delivered to adorn the main pool overlooking a private pond, he spent the rest of the afternoon having the delivery men position it. "A little to the left. A little more to the left. Now to the right. What if we turn it around." His type of wealth needs tending to, no matter whose back is breaking to facilitate it.

James, the family's event coordinator, wears an earpiece and carries a tablet while managing the staff for a gathering of guests to greet the Rotterdams upon their arrival. On the grounds in the back, Chinese acrobats climbing a stack of twenty-five chairs culminates into a triple backflip into the waiting arms of their comrades.

The Rotterdams join James outside on the veranda. "These little yellow acrobats are so...twisty," Annesley says, puckering her lips as she makes spinny motions with her hands.

"We should make them fight." Laughton throws his silver martini pick in their general direction, finishes his drink, then throws his glass.

Vanessa asks, "What have we here, James?"

James is naturally excited to please. "Golden Dragon Acrobats. They were sent over by the Prime Minister. There's tea later and then bocce with members from the club."

"Sounds exhausting," she slumps and takes her leave of the festivities, retreating to her all-white boudoir, her nearly fulltime haven. She begins her beauty regimen that entails laying in an Amazonian rock crystal tub filled with royal jelly. When she's done soaking, she passes marble countertops and white lacquer cabinets on her long walk to shower the thick, waxy substance dripping off of her.

A freshly cleansed Vanessa lays back on her immaculate, like-it's-never-been-slept-in bed and turns on her gold plated tablet to watch Bava, an online guru on Topp App.

The intro begins with Bava flying over the world on a yoga mat, over waterfalls and lush valleys, waving to everybody as he flies over, before settling down into a lotus position. "Greetings, dear ones. Welcome to Manisha. A place of learning. We are family. We are one. I am grateful to be your guide. I am Bava." The melodious wah-wah of a Tibetan singing bowl resonates from somewhere offstage. "Today friends, we are going to talk about the culture of greed, of always wanting more. It is an ever increasingly shallow downward trajectory to allow yourself to be manipulated into the worship of material things. If you allow yourself to be seduced by the cult of greed, you open your heart chakra to the evil of believing that only outside forces and things can fulfill you. Wasteful luxury is a costly and empty endeavor that seems to have no end. When is enough enough?

"Be like the sage that remains still unless required to move in the service of others. Awaken in you only a form of enlightenment that enhances humanity's allowance for truth, beauty, love, and understanding, that which is required of you to make this journey worthy of you as a sentient being of pure light as you contribute to the balance of the universe. Maintaining that balance requires living not in excess but in goodness, showing the same amount of care and attention towards everyone, so that future generations may also have the same degree of happiness and comfort as you pass along the teachings that honor the sacred energy that makes our very existence possible."

Dr. Harlan Braun wears a Hazmat suit in a lab at Paradigm Solutions. Hundreds of thousands of mosquitoes crowd the transparent lucite trays, the overwhelming sound of buzzing permeates the room.

A phone drone interrupts Braun's work. Lab technicians duck as it flies dangerously close to their heads. Amschel's eyes appear on the narrow screen as the phone drone circles Braun. "Good afternoon, sir!" Braun's thick German accent is muffled from the helmet.

"Braun! What's with the suit? You look like a fire hydrant. Take that damn thing off so I can hear you."

"But sir, it's a safety precaution."

"I couldn't give a fig," says Amschel. Braun takes off the helmet, revealing a face deeply lined from years of scrutiny. "Where are we with the next batch? We are expecting a forty-eight-hour life span this time, one hundred percent lethality. And talk to me about regeneration. We're still scheduled to send them out pregnant, yes?"

Braun is quick to reply. "In a vurd, sir, yes. Vee are very confident vee vill hit all of our parameters. Penetrating all but commercial grade beekeeping fabric. Vee vill be sending out eighty percent impregnated females. And zey vill be hungry!"

Amschel sits at his desk near a Jacobean Oak Fireplace, ablaze beneath an 18th century painting of figures admiring a cavernous interior dripping with stalactites. He wears Virtual Reality glasses while piloting the phone drone simulator using a desktop joystick. "Show me production."

"Of course, sir. Right zees vay." Braun guides the phone drone through the lab to the pools, a brewery like room with huge gestation vats. The six-foot by twenty-feet shallow pools are filled with specialized eggs. Sun lamps hang above them to create a natural habitat.

Amschel flies the phone drone closer to get a better look inside. "And how many can you brew per batch?"

"Seventy kilos per metric ton."

"How many, in English? Full capacity."

"Ten million a day, sir."

"Good. I'll alert the partners. Carry on." Amschel removes the VR glasses, thinking he's hung up the phone drone. "Vile little troll," he says and rejoins the party being thrown in his home.

Braun hears his comment and his face falls. Taking off his hazmat suit, he talks to himself. "Call me a little troll. I'm an inch and a half taller zan you!" He retreats to his office, a framed black and white picture of a man in a Nazi uniform is the only personal item in his office. "Troll? I have six degrees in three languages, troll! I'm changing zee vorld for you! You are zee troll! You don't understand vut I do. Inbred ingrate!"

Mills is shooting some baskets on the Nest's court, the one place he can be alone to center his thoughts. Bishop knows this and it's the first place he looks for him. "It's about go time, John."

"I'm not sure I can do it anymore."

"This is not a repeat of the last time. It's imperative you stay away from Blackwell or risk blowing our cover. Under no circumstances can he know you're still alive."

Mills nods his head. "So, where to?"

Bishop takes a seat on a bench by the court and motions for Mills to join him. "I need to warn you about our target. Dr. Harlan Braun has been used by the Order for years to carry out research for the Department of Security, a cover for creating weapons for killing innocent people. And because their funds are unlimited, their scope is unprecedented. Braun was chosen because of who his father was, Dr. Erich Braun, the director of the Third Reich's virological and bacteriological warfare program. Project Paperclip brought Nazi scientists to America after the war, after which Plum Island Animal Disease Center was established, a secret U.S. biological warfare program. They experimented with, among other things, ticks dropped from planes carrying Lyme Disease to see if they were a viable method for biological warfare."

Bishop feels the gravity of what he's asking of Mills and wrings his hands. "John, you have to know someone's motivations in order to influence them. Braun was inspired at a very young age to pursue the most horribly imaginative weapons for purely destructive purposes. We need to know what their next plan of attack is. Skid Row was the start of something big and we need to be prepared. Get the lay of the land. Give us audible of what you see and hear. Find the target. Braun is the Director of this whole operation. Get as close to him as possible but be careful. If it feels organic, penetrate."

Mills takes a seat in a makeshift lab at the Nest with Leland at his side and Bishop looking on. "Remember this, old friend?" Leland says, hooking him up to the heart monitor.

"Tough to forget."

"I'm going to give you the coordinates of Paradigm Solutions. Not that you'll need it."

"It's been so long I'll be surprised if I can make it off this base."

Bishop starts the metronome. Mills closes his eyes and is able to locate the target with ease. He is Remote Viewing the tanks and the pools filled with eggs, reporting what he sees as Leland takes notes. The mention of the mosquitoes is a reminder of the Beta test on Skid Row, confirming they are on the right track. "Keep going, Milly," Leland says.

Braun is sitting at his desk in his office, as Mills enters the room and takes a look around. He sees the Nazi photograph and it gives him an idea. But before he can begin his process of Remote Influencing, Braun looks up, recognizing a presence. "Vat have vee here? Someone comes to play baby games? You come to me vith zis? I know vut zis is." Braun begins laughing. "I know you're zere, coming to me vith your baby games. Ahhh, vee did dis in camp in our seventh year, like shooing away a fly." Braun laughs louder, shutting his mind down as an ironclad fortress. "I know all zee ways you can create an illusion. I vas trained for zis. I am a master, you fool! Do you not know who my father vas? Who he vurked for?" The laughing stops and his voice turns sinister. "Now let's find out who you are. Vut is your name, little baby games?"

Mills backs away from him.

Braun pouts. "No fair. You know who I am. But I can't know who you are?"

Mills pulls the shoot and snaps back to the Nest.

Leland is surprised by his sudden return. "That was fast."

"He won't let me in. He knew I was there, son of a bitch was laughing at me. He's fortified, man. Master of his domain." Mills is shaken like he just got caught stealing. "I don't know if I have what it takes to do this anymore."

Bishop's approach is gentle. "Don't worry, John.

99

We'll stop them. One way or another. Just relax and detox."

Amschel boards a shiny black S-92 helicopter from the North end of Doden Hall, the interior bestrewn in gold and crystal. He phones Blackwell. "Tell the partners we're ready to start shipping heavy. Is everything in place?"

"We're nailed down. The media briefs are queued and the vaccines are stockpiled, ready for distribution."

"Good, we'll start with cleaning up the Capital. It's a fucking disgrace."

The chopper circles Santa Catalina Island, twenty-two miles off the coast of Los Angeles, locating the private helipad attached to an illustrious mansion positioned at the apex of the rocky coastline of Mount Ada, with 360-degree panoramic views of the ocean. The Patriarch, an old-school traditionalist accountable to no one, insisted that this was where he could do his best thinking. The steel walls embedded into the mountainside surround and protect the fortress without blocking the view from the master bedroom located on the top floor, under an elegant Victorian turret.

Trained personnel are eager to greet the prodigal son. "Welcome to Aegis, sir!"

Amschel scoffs, murmuring under his cultured British breath, "Ghastly."

The Patriarch's room is littered with sculptures, fine art, and every kind of advanced life support machine known to modern science. His unwillingness to die has turned him severely rotten, his appearance that of a damaged peach. The true enablers are the doctors keeping him alive, at his insistence. He maintains a staunch belief that the decisions he makes today will better serve the best of mankind tomorrow. "The prospect of a decent life on our planet is threatened with increased life expectancy and a decline in infant mortality rate. Population needs to be stabilized or else there will be a catastrophic disaster to the biosphere we live in," he is known to say in public. But in private, his tongue grows much sharper. "Cattle to be herded and led to the slaughter." The Patriarch and his cronies put into place all of the initial poisons. The rich, they claim, are cognitively superior to the poor, who are unable to handle the magnitude of such issues. The Patriarch then handed the baton to his son, who follows orders to stay in good graces, his inheritance on the line.

A full staff handles the old man's every need. Unfortunate for them, as the old man is twice the bastard he once was due to his advanced age. Those surrounding him are paid handsomely to jump at his every request, and as a master manipulator, the demand is high and constant. The huge burden on his employees is such that you cannot ever please the Patriarch, but he will make you cry trying.

As Amschel enters the grand room, the Patriarch is terrifying a young nurse with his shrieks. "I said get out of here, goddamn it!" he yells at the top of his lungs with a voice raspy and damaged with practice. She rushes out of the room in tears.

Uly, the head nurse, is quick to greet him. A fleshy, effeminate man who hasn't lost his sense of humor, Uly has been with the Patriarch the longest. He decided long ago not to take this shit personally.

"Oh, he's in a mood today. Good to see you Amschel. Right this way," he says softly, with a warm smile. In addition to the armed security guard outside the room, Uly's main job is to monitor the life support system control panel from his station on the opposite side of the room.

Enclosing the bed are multiple computer monitors, high-tech weather scopes, and a large computer interface. The Patriarch operates his entire empire from the confines of his bed. A gray-bearded man on the largest screen speaks in Russian, his transmission being translated in real time. "We have the necessary tankers to keep in motion. We now have four complete submarine crews ready to deploy. Our passenger list has been reviewed and authorized."

"This would have been great news a week ago, but as it stands, you're still jeopardizing your own personal seat at the table. There's no margin for error. You Cossacks are useful but easily replaced. "

The man on the screen responds, "Is that all for

now, sir?"

The Patriarch pushes a button on the remote held by his frail hand, his shrunken body attached to a myriad of tubes. "Mongrel beef-wit," he spits.

Amschel nears the bed and peers at his father's ravaged body. "You're looking well, father," he manages.

"Don't be glib. What have you loused up now?"

Amschel grits his teeth. "Beta was a success, by all accounts. Approximately ten-thousand undesirables eradicated."

The Patriarch is not at all happy with the numbers. "Bollocks! For that kind of exposure, we expected five times that! The level to which you disappoint me is infinite. You possess no gumption, nor skill. Pray you never have to compete in the real world, you embossed carbuncle."

"Braun is preparing a new batch for the next round as we speak."

"Well, what are you waiting for? Stop wasting my time and get me the numbers I asked for!" The Patriarch calls to his attendant. "Uly! That is all."

Amschel is ushered out by the security guard. He boards his S-92 and sits back on the tan, soft leather seat, exhaling deeply. He pulls from inside his jacket pocket a long, silver cigarette case housing high-grade pharmaceutical needles. *I loathe him with the heat of a trillion suns.* He squirts liquid from one of the needles into the air to clear any bubbles and administers the medicine directly into his neck. He takes a deep breath and holds it, loosening his tie. When his riled nerves have cooled, he expertly licks the tip of the syringe and returns the needle to the silver case, tucking it back into his jacket pocket.

He places a call. "Braun, Operation Alpha. Make it happen. Tonight."

"Payload arrived in D.C. moments ago, sir. Zee CAV is on standby. However, zay are expecting rain and vind. I advise against zis as we've been informed by National Shield zee veather vill not permit a perfect launch."

Amschel steamrolls him. "Who said anything about perfect? Make it happen, you gnashnab!"

A C17 military cargo plane taxis away from the large green crate left on the tarmac. The ground crew of the District of Columbia Bulwark Air Base works quickly under the night sky, removing the cinching metal cables off the top of the crate, unearthing the rugged transport case inside. A Cargo Air Vehicle, or CAV, is wheeled into place, powered by an electric propulsion system, and outfitted with eight rotors allowing for vertical flight. Following strict orders, the ground crew stores the case in the CAV's payload pod. They slide a protective cover panel on the side of the transport case, revealing a keypad. A numbered sequence engages the timed release chute on the triggered bottom of the case. Signaling to base, the propellers are ignited and the autonomous CAV shoots straight up, equipped with the cluster bomb of mosquitoes underneath.

Top of his class, Pocket is a slender introvert of just twenty, his skin pale from too many hours indoors. He is considered by many to be an intelligence specialist. Prior to logging over five thousand hours of flight time, he became a proficient remotely-piloted-aircraft sensor operator, controlling the cameras, lasers and other information-gathering equipment on unmanned aircraft used in operational tactics. He is brought in to fly the CAV for Operation Alpha because he's the best and brightest they've got.

Pocket is ushered into Briefing Room #3 for a pre-shift mission meeting to go over his orders. An operations officer wearing a regulation green flight suit is taking him through it, scrawling logistics on a whiteboard behind him. Pocket pays close attention to the target location: low-income housing projects North of the Capital. He receives no further details of why this target was chosen. He tries to make sense of the lack of information he's being given about why he's been brought here, other than he'll have to fly this CAV over secured air space. A screen projects the currents skies, cloudy with low visibility. He will essentially be flying blind, but the officer assures him he's the man for the job. He thinks something doesn't feel right about this.

The officer closes his metal binder and steps out

to speak with an MP waiting by the door. Pocket uses the cover of his own body to slide his device out of his jumper and enter into an encrypted game chat the coordinates of the designated target with the word BEFORE and the longitude and latitude of a different location with the word AFTER. He deftly slides his device back into place.

Pocket is led into a control room buzzing with active duty members cross-checking data from metal binders. A safety inspector hovers to ensure the payload drop goes by the book. Men in dark suits at the top of the food chain of command stand in the back of the room in quiet observation.

He takes a seat on a padded cockpit chair, multiple video inputs stacked on top of each other in front of him. A military grade LCD monitor displays night vision goggle-compatible aerial surveillance of the target location, high-performance video controllers at the ready. He puts on a headset and awaits countdown.

Elijah, a Rogue member of the Amorphous Cell operating out of an abandoned warehouse in an industrial part of Downtown LA, receives the message on his encrypted gaming console. "Pocket, my man!"

He calls over a fellow Rogue named Malakai. "Watch and learn, my friend." Malakai takes a seat and watches as Elijah gets to work on his secured desktop. "All wireless devices have the same vulnerabilities. We have to send the correct spoofing signals so that they reach the receiver at the right time." He types 'airmon-ng start' in white letters onto a black screen, putting his card into monitor mode. "After Pocket synchronizes to the legitimate GPS service to lock onto our spoofing signal, we can take over the satellite lock without the constraint of triggering the fault detector." The black screen fills with code. Then it clears and he types in 'airmon-ng check kill' to end any interfering processes. "Pocket's location will receive legitimate GPS signals when the spoofing attack starts. We then create GPS spoofing signals by decoding the legitimate GPS signals and create time-shifted copies which are transmitted with higher energy to overpower the original signals using pulse-delaying navigation signals and switch the lock from the legitimate GPS signal to our spoofing signal without detection. We then add the new coordinates he sent and blamo! Seamless satellite-lock takeover." Data starts compiling on the screen. The screen asks to de-authenticate the target permanently. He fills in a long code comprised of multiple combinations of letters and numbers.

Elijah's device displays a blue screen, awaiting his command. "Now we connect to the target with our cracked phone with enabled protections to control the drone." He virtually disconnects Pocket's screen, slides down a window, and pushes a button connecting the device. The screen on his device goes black, then the sharp contrast of the image from Pocket's monitor reflecting D.C. at night through infrared imaging fills the frame. "Woo hoo! Let's go for a swim."

The CAV flies over the ghettos of Washington D.C. under the cover of night. The payload drop is in the initial stages of deployment as hundreds of the mosquitoes are starting to be released, but the CAV is quickly redirected into the Potomac and sunk.

The control room is up in arms. The operations officers are questioning Pocket and he is unable to provide answers. "No idea what happened, sir. The bird was no longer under my control."

The fraction of mosquitoes to touch ground swarm a young black mother walking her baby in a stroller, a group of black teens playing basketball under a street lamp adjacent to their tenement building, and a few overworked people getting on a local bus. The swarm follows the people onto the bus, attacking those onboard. Their screams are ruinous.

Breaking news: "Good evening, ladies and gentlemen. Reilly Williams reporting live from the studio on an outbreak in D.C. There's an apparent strain of East Asian Encephalitis being carried by swarms of mosquitoes, unlike anything we've ever seen before. Areas reporting cases so far: Columbia Heights, Petworth, and Shaw. These ghettos, uh neighborhoods, are in the Northwest area of D.C. It's fast-acting and undeniably deadly. Fortunately, there is a vaccine. The

folks over at Paradigm Solutions anticipated the outbreak. They're shipping in emergency vaccinations
right now that can be picked up at your local phar-
macy. For those in need, emergency credit is available
through Red Cross monetary fund at the low price of
eighteen percent interest. Back after break."

They go to sponsor and Reilly Williams turns
to a black production assistant with a headset and
a clipboard, "Gosh, I hope none of your family was
hurt."

"I'm from Connecticut, asshole," she says under
her breath.

Blackwell's black chopper touches down on the
airstrip at Doden Hall. A barrage of security shows
him in and as he waits for Amschel to grace his presence, the youngest of the Rotterdam Clan, Winnie, returns from her morning tennis lesson, rosy with flush.

Drinking down a glass of juice in the kitchen,
Blackwell pounces. "Practicing your backswing? Wow,
you're getting a lot of sun." He touches her shoulders,
causing her to recoil. He licks his fingers. "You taste
like a baby kitten smothered in butterscotch," he says,
swirling the whiskey he helped himself to.

Amschel enters the room in high spirits and
greets Blackwell. "Winnie, go tell Thelma we're ready
for breakfast. Run along." She is all too happy to remove herself from Blackwell's presence.

They sit at a table with enough food for ten men

and await the final tally. The video call comes in on a monitor inset into the wall in the dining hall, normally hidden behind a Gauguin. "What are the numbers on the event? How many did we get?" Amschel asks as eager as he'll ever be, using the side of a small spoon to crack open a soft-boiled egg resting in a vintage floral moss rose egg cup.

"Twenty-eight, sir," Braun reports, his voice cracking.

"Twenty-eight thousand! Brilliant! That's better than expected."

"No, sir, twenty-eight. Twenty-eight casualties."

"That's preposterous. We employed ten times more mosquitoes than our Beta test Downtown."

"Like I tried to point out to you, sir, it vus not advisable to launch during inclement veather. Vind velocity redirected all but four percent of our assets.

"This is not going to be the media event we'd hoped for," Amschel says without emotion.

Blackwell reassures him while stuffing a large croissant in his mouth smothered in hand-seeded red currant jam. "We can spin it in the media. Make it bigger. We're exempt from disclosure. A thousand deaths are enough to move a lot of vaccines."

Amschel affects a waxy smile. "Life is always unpredictable. That's what gives it joi de vivre."

The IGA is buzzing from last night's event in D.C. Amir is at his desk and receives a notification signaling him to join the Amorphous Cell in the sub-level below. He turns off his monitor and leaves his post immediately, disappearing behind a corridor. A beautiful Asian junior intern stationed nearby, Connie, watches him go, taking note.

The members of the Amorphous Cell are busy studying the Alpha event, watching multiple angles from nearby CCTV cameras in the area while collecting feedback from the recorded transmissions of witnesses at the various locations the mosquitoes actually touched ground, uncovering as many details as they can.

With multiple screens displaying Intel at once, Amir checks the time and flips yet another screen on to broadcast the Jack Hammer Show, led by a bombastic, ruddy-faced man full of bravado and whiskey. His animated fast talker schtick is not unlike a coked-up car salesman, but his guests are worth the hassle.

The interview underway is with the head of the Keepers, Mountain Macoy, a barrel-chested, silver-back gorilla of a man in his healthy fifties, his large, ruggedly handsome head and strong chin matches his frame. He is a man of action, with piercing blue eyes that carry sorrowed determination. Speaking in a deep register, his words convey quiet deliberation. "The Keepers are wholeheartedly against any and all government sponsored microwaved manipulation of its citizens. When 5G cell towers were introduced on every lamppost, utility pole, home, and business throughout entire neighborhoods, towns and cities, the dangers of their ultra high frequency and intensity quickly became apparent. If you think about it, earlier generations were already showing signs of being problematic and they had a frequency between one and four gigahertz. 5G uses between twenty-three to ninety gigahertz. That's ninety billion electromagnetic radiation waves disrupting the cellular mechanism of every organ of the body each second. The damage to bee colonies has been astronomical. The magnetite in their bodies to guide them home is disrupted by the wavelengths of these information-carrying radio waves and the bees aren't able to make it back to their hives. And they die in droves. This is largely why we live off the grid. We know it's better for our bodies and better for our minds."

In the studio, Jack Hammer speaks to Mountain from behind his desk in traditional interview fashion, yet both men sit back in their chairs in an atmosphere that feels more relaxed than his usual hand-to-the-fire mode of questioning.

Jack Hammer plays devil's advocate. "Whoa, Kemosabe. You're telling me the government has allowed this technology to be forced on people without their knowledge or consent without proving its safety? The telecom industry isn't even aware of the adverse effects themselves?

"That is correct."

"Well, there you have it, folks. People over profits,

once again. Reckless in the extreme."

"It becomes a matter of liberty over tyranny."

The producers interrupt Jack Hammer through his earpiece. "I understand we have an expert on the line, someone who has worked intimately with this technology. Go ahead, you're on the air. Hello? What's your name, sir?"

The voice on the other end of the line is one of calm detachment. "I can't tell you my name, but I can tell you I've been involved in designing aspects of this technology for the Department of Security for over thirty years. What you're saying is true, but the technology has far surpassed expectations and it's much more malevolent than you can imagine. This is classified information and representatives from the most powerful first-world countries worldwide are involved."

Jack Hammer slaps the table. "Ok, Matador. Let's say you're right. What's the ultimate goal here? What are they after?"

"Culling the population. It's been recently revealed to me my work will enable evil men to do terrible things. Technology is inherently indifferent. Depending on whose side you're on, it can be used for good or evil. The Sound of God Weapon is a complex technology involving bioelectric magnetic neuroscience that will be broadcast across regions of the country, causing extreme pain then imminent death for those in its path. This is all part of their strategy to control dissenters and thin the herd. A campaign of genocide."

"So, you know for a fact this will be used on American soil?"

"For decades, the DoS has been experimenting on the unwitting population through a series of maneuvers, modified titles, and increasingly bigger budgets. But this latest move will far surpass anything that's been done before."

"And the Order is behind this."

"Yes. They are a select group of people behind our governments with the money and the power to make decisions for the rest of us on a global scale. These are in no way elected officials."

"How can they be stopped?"

"They operate out of sight, free to act as they please while taking advantage of our servitude."

"How are you speaking to us right now? Are you still involved in the program?"

"After discovering they were to use it against the citizens of our country, I have been operating against my will."

"Are you in danger?"

"It's not important what happens to me. The public needs to know what their intentions are. The Order must be stopped."

"Aren't you scared?"

"Shakespeare said a coward dies many deaths, the noble die but once. Death should not be what we're afraid of, but of our complicity in the triumph of evil."

"Do they have a target in mind?"

"I'm afraid they do. And the attack is forthcoming." The sound of approaching footsteps can be heard in the background. The phone goes dead.

Jack Hammer and Mountain are left speechless. When he finds his voice again, Jack Hammer says, "Well, that was an education in courage. You've got to dare great in order to make a difference. Prayers for our brothers and sisters who possess the strength to speak out on behalf of all of us. Please keep them safe."

5. Cold Creek Ranch

In the alpine meadows and valley grasslands of Southwest Montana, fondly resembling the American frontier of the 1880s, is a collection of log cabins, windmills, wells, and modestly dressed people going about their daily lives, using horse-drawn tillage on their resilient farming homesteads. The happy faces of children communing with nature, sun on their little faces and wind in their silk spun hair, complete this beautiful utopian landscape.

The Keepers are brave ex-servicemen and women who fight for the Constitution. They know how to organize. They know how to live off the land. They take shit from no one and that makes them dangerous to the Order. Turner Boone, real estate mogul billionaire on the right side of history, welcomed them when the time came to take matters into their own hands and they've been here ever since.

A church bell sounds a distress alarm in the distance, disrupting the blessed tranquility. Men, women, and children drop what they're doing and run or ride swiftly towards the center of what constitutes their town, a collection of wooden structures arranged in a horseshoe-like fashion, including a blacksmith, a furrier, dry food storage, and horse troughs. All the buildings are being manned by figures with rifles. The cellar doors built into the structures fly open to accommodate the women, children, and pets. Everyone moves in silence.

The last of the settlers find refuge as the church bell ceases and with it, the awareness of a whiny, buzzing noise from above. From high in the sky, a bird of prey swoops down and dives sharply, slamming into a drone that has entered its airspace. Its leather and steel-armored talons grab hold of it tightly, trained to keep these unwanted birds out of the food chain. The hawk gives a piercing shriek and delivers the drone directly to Mountain, a leather gauntlet protecting his left arm, a walkie-talkie in his right. From horseback, he motions to the mounted cavalry behind him and they ride together to bring it in.

Watching the drill unfold from the vantage point of a high plateau is Turner Boone, a rugged man donning a silver moustache and a beaver skin Stetson. He surveys the scene through binoculars from atop his grey gelding, checks his watch, and puts a Bobby Whistle to his lips, issuing forth two blasts, taking a single deep breath for each one.

Wabash Cavenaugh, a robust man in his forties with wild eyes and hair, is hunkered down behind a sandbag bunker scanning the foreground with a scoped rifle. He hears Boone's whistle and starts the chain reaction of "All Clear" hand signals down the line of drill-ready Keepers. Wabash and the others hop on their horses and break into a gallop down the butte towards town.

Boone watches them go and turns to his guest,

118

also atop a steed, and smiles proudly. "They're a randy bunch, but they know how to mobilize. Been a long time since most of 'em had anything to call their own. Community can be an awesome force." His gravelly voice has a distinctive quality to it.

"Seeing it with my own eyes does not disappoint. Well done, old friend," Bishop says, regarding Boone with a tip of his beat-up cowboy hat.

They head down to meet the others at the Lodge. Upon arriving, Boone warmly greets the assembled inhabitants of Cold Creek Ranch. Mountain spots their entrance and takes long strides to meet them at the door. "Bishop! How're things down at the Nest?"

"It's going noble."

"Legacies are earned, my friend," he says with a broad smile. They embrace.

Women in jeans and cotton flannel shirts serve coffee alongside men and women in tactical gear with agendas on clipboards. People mill about, conversing with one another in a warm, neighborly fashion, their fellowship tightly knit.

Boone takes to the pulpit at the front of the room. "Ladies and gentlemen, I'd like to start today's meeting by introducing our special guest Joseph Bishop. He's been an advocate for the people and a defender of natural law since our days at West Point." Bishop smiles and gives a quick wave. "Today's drill reflects your determination and hard-won preparation. I am so proud to call you my brothers and sisters." Boone turns the meeting over to Mountain.

"We, the Keepers, have pledged to fulfill the oath that our military and law enforcement brothers and sisters take to defend the Constitution against all enemies, foreign and domestic. Men and women have fought and bled and died for freedom. They gave us a valuable oath knowing it could mean their life. Now's it's our turn to make sure the light of liberty must never go out. All that matters is that our children remain free when it's our time to go.

"Our Founding Fathers established a Nation to protect individual freedom from those that wish to enslave us. Your efforts continue to steel our resolve to do what's right in support of this Declaration and affirm our sacred trust to each other to protect our lives and our honor above all else. There has only ever been one battle: The battle between people who seek to control others and those of us who wish to be left alone. The Order wants us to think it's hopeless. They want to keep us enslaved. Not on our watch. Do not let fear control you. Relentless tyranny will continue unless it is met with coordinated legion."

Freshly made applesauce cake is being served before a blazing stone fireplace in the Lodge while Bishop, Boone, and Mountain sit outside on the porch, smoking pipes while rocking in chairs.

Bishop remains calm but vigilant. "They call it the Sound of God Weapon. Initially, isolated neural monitoring was used by the Order through a microwave tower network leftover from the cold war to influence targeted individuals. People reported feeling headaches, loss of memory, false Alzheimer's diagnosis, and receptivity to programming. From recent reports, it looks as if they've expanded their capabilities to include inflammation of the brain to the point of death and their scope can affect large groups en masse.

"We know Matador is being held at the Dulce Base compound and we have the schematics to penetrate it. Over the years, the Amorphous Cell has been devising back doors into their systems, giving us the ability to control nearly every aspect of their security complex. We know where all guards are stationed and when. We can falsify a drill and can unlock gates and open the right doors. We don't need to go in heavy, just a few good men." Bishop pauses for a moment to take in the beautiful mountainous scenery. When he continues, he is solemn. "Matador is the only one who had the guts to come forward on this. And there's a chance he might know how to stop it. We need your help getting him out. That is, if he isn't dead already."

"Whatever it takes to stop the gluttonous oligarchs. Thank god I had the moral compass not to become one of them," Boone says.

Mountain offers his hand. "Sacrifice has always been a part of our creed." Bishop shakes it.

Early the next day, Bishop boards a Janet plane out of Billings and heads to Dulce, New Mexico. With him are Mountain, Wabash and two strong but silent Keepers, muscles taught for action. Once they've touched down at Aztec Municipal Airport, Keepers brethren pick them up in two government surplus vehicles to cover the remaining distance. They secure a position outside the facility, just out of sight. Mountain and Wabash are in one vehicle with a walkie talkie and their backup, Bishop is in the second vehicle with the others and an open laptop revealing a map of the inner workings of the secret lab sent over to him by Amir.

The Amorphous Cell stands by as they prepare for the siege on the fortified laboratory complex. With no time to waste, Bishop authorizes them to set off multiple alarms, alerting personnel within Paradigm Solutions of a high-level security drill.

Braun is in his lab, testing the Sound of God Weapon on innocent chimpanzees behind sound-proofed, protective glass. As he increases the wave, the monkeys begin to stir, holding their heads, and try desperately to get out of the room. The pain in their skulls becomes too intense. They fall to the ground and start convulsing.

Braun takes notes. "Ah, zis is a full three minutes faster zan last time. Look at zem. Wow. The grand mal seizure has exceeded my expectations. Wow.

122

Make a note. Next time we put a microphone in za room so we can hear za sounds," he says, addressing his lab assistant.

They are interrupted by a blaring siren. His assistant gets a notification on his computer monitor, shutting him out from their work at hand. "Sir, it's a Code Red Emergency. It's coming from the very top of Strategic Command."

"Well, turn it off. Zis lab is autonomous. Vee should have full control."

"I'm sorry, sir. I can't. It's restricting my access. The only option it's giving me is to exit the program."

"Impossible. Get up!"

He pushes his assistant out of the way and takes position in front of the screen. He pushes several buttons to override the system. When that doesn't work, he curses in German. "Wertlos verdammten narren!" His eyes bulge, the veins popping out of his neck.

Inside the Incident Control Room, the Security Manager cross-checks the feed. "They're calling for a Total Lockdown. I've never seen this done before," he says to the other guard, searching a metal file cabinet for the manual. Flipping through the Disaster Notification and Mobilization Procedure, he finds the Total Lockdown protocols and reads aloud. "Establishing a secure perimeter and the routing of foot and vehicular traffic to control entry/exit points that are staffed by security and/or facility personnel are key elements in controlling and maintaining the integrity of the facility and its surrounding perimeter. Lock down all weapons and get to emergency posts until further instructed." He looks up from the manual. "These guys must be running some serious maneuvers. Ok, according to this, we have six minutes to activate a Rapid Response Team and get all technicians and personnel down into the bunker or we fail." He announces via overhead paging "Code Red is now in effect" three times. "Guards are instructed to take their post at emergency stations."

"What about the prisoner?"

"He's already secure."

The call comes in to the main post at the gate. "Close up the mountain. Nobody gets in or out." The sound of the critical emergency horn blasts through the mountainside as the guards close the steel vault door and lock it, returning to their posts.

Braun marches over to the Incident Command Center, his assistant at his heels. "I am in zee middle of testing. Shut zat blasted alarm off now!"

"We have our orders. We have to protect the data," the Security Manager says.

Braun is incredulous. "I can't be expected to follow zees rules."

"I'm sorry, sir. You have to come with us. It is our duty to establish emergency lockdown security measures to ensure the safety and security of everyone in this facility. Provisions will be provided." Guards usher Braun and his assistant down the bland, luminescent hallways to an elevator that takes them from the third sublevel down to the fifth sublevel to a small, secure bunker.

The safe room is submarine tight, lined with long, white cafeteria tables with attached benches. After the allotted time, the hacked system freezes all doors to the battle stations, locking them in place. Scientists and security personnel mill about as attendants begin serving stale cookies on styrofoam plates and apple juice from concentrate in tiny, plastic cups.

Braun takes a seat on a bench and scowls. His assistant joins him with two plates of the meager offerings and cups of watered-down coffee. Braun waves it off. "A viable explanation for ven vee release such a weapon could entail a direct-hit coronal mass ejection zat biologically affects brain activity, sense of equilibrium, and zee central nervous system, causing intracranial pressure and death by cerebral edema."

Bishop instructs Leland back at the Nest to activate Mills, who is standing by to address the guards posted at the front gate, effectively securing the only road in. Within minutes, the guards have left their command post to unlock the main gate, then drop to the ground and start doing pushups, sounding off.

Mountain and his team drive slowly past the gate towards a road flanked on either side by eight feet high Cyclone fencing stacked with barbed wire, the only path into the belly of the beast. They enter the fortified structure through the open mouth of the cave and disappear down the tunnel.

They park their vehicle near the sealed vault door. The Amorphous Cell triggers the lock, revealing a ghost town behind it. "We're in," Mountain says into his walkie. "Now what?"

Bishop guides them by walkie down long corridors, doors unlocking before them as they approach, to an elevator. Once inside, the elevator panel displays innumerable sublevels continuing deep underground. "Where to?" Mountain says, barely above a whisper.

"Can we say hi to the aliens?" Wabash asks, lacking an inside voice.

Mountain puts his finger to his lips. The elevator is tripped and takes them to the third sub-level. Guns drawn, they disembark with caution towards the tracking device Amir has accessed reflecting an RFID chip that's been logged into the system as belonging to Digby Lange. They get to the door of the room the signal is coming from and there is a thick padlock on it. "I've got some bad news," Mountain says into the walkie.

Wabash holds up his hand. "On it. Step back, fellas." He produces C-4 from his pocket with a shit-eating grin on his face, like a kid excited to play with a dangerous toy. He calls through the door. "Mr. Lange? Are you in there?"

Digby is sitting on the other side of the door on a steel cot. He looks up, fearful to respond. "Hello?"

126

"There is about to be a concussive force on this door. I need you to move as far away from it as possible. Can you do that?"

Digby hesitates and manages, "I think so." He walks to the back of the room, huddles in the corner, and covers his ears.

"Great. We're going to get you out of here," Wabash speaks from years of proficiency in blowing things up. He fashions the makeshift bomb using putty and wires. When it's ready, they duck for cover.

The bomb goes off, the sound echoing through the hallways. The chimpanzees housed in the nearby lab start grunting and screeching, drumming on their cages with the flat of their hands. "Jesus, that was loud. We have to hurry," Mountain says. When the smoke clears, they storm the room.

Digby slowly stands, uncovering his ears.

"Dr. Lange. Mountain Macoy. We were on the Jack Hammer Show together. Big fan of your work. You wanna get out of here?"

"I need my case. We can't leave without it."

The vibration from the bomb can be felt in the bunker. Braun stands, alerted. "Did you hear zat? Did anyone hear zat? Zis is not a fucking drill."

The security guards look around, alarmed. They attempt to open the door using their passkeys and are unable to. Panic spreads quickly.

"Dis isn't right. You should be able to open every

door. Vut is really going on here?"

"Sir, we'll get to the bottom of this, I assure you."

"Shoot zee door!" Braun yells. "Our research is in danger of exposure!" The security guards stand around sheepishly, looking at one another. "I am zee Executive Director of zis facility. Do it on my authority and do it now!"

A guard steps up, takes aim, and shoots. The bullet ricochets off the metal lock and the people inside the bunker scream, dropping to the floor.

"Give me zat!" Braun grabs the guard's automatic rifle. He aims around the lock and squeezes a barrage of bullets, releasing a full clip. He kicks the demolished door open and runs towards the elevator, the guards following close behind.

The Keepers follow Digby to the lab and find the door locked. Mountain reaches out to Bishop. "Small pickup. We need you to open Biotech Lab 3." The message is passed on and Amir trips the lock.

Digby races to his office connected to the lab and searches everywhere for his case. "It's not here," he says. They scour the main lab. The sound of rapid gunfire is heard on a sublevel below them. The chimpanzees' howls are ear-piercing, putting the men on edge. Digby spots the case hidden in the corner under some heavy equipment and the men frantically help him dig it out. They free the case and sprint towards the elevator and upon reaching it, they see that it is traveling down to the fifth sublevel.

Braun and the guards have summoned the elevator, taking note that it was resting on the third sub-level. The wait is excruciating for Braun, his precious lab potentially compromised.

The elevator arrives and they get in.

Mountain gets on the walkie fast. "We're not the only ones moving down here. How many ways to the surface?"

Bishop scrambles to find a stairwell on the map. "Go back the way you came, make your first left, then another left, and it's the fourth door on the left. Emergency stairwell, single file."

"Got it."

When they get to the door, they hear the click of the tripped lock and they open it, taking the narrow stairwell up. Digby struggles with the case. Mountain scoops it up and throws it over his wide back with ease.

The door at the top of the stairs clicks and they pull it open, running as fast as they can towards the exit.

Braun and his men are nearing the third sublevel and the elevator stops short. They push the several buttons and nothing happens. They are stuck. "Sohn einer Hure!" Braun shouts, his bug eyes bulging.

Bishop sees the military vehicle exit the mouth of the facility and he breathes a sigh of relief. The Keepers deliver Digby to him but before they can move,

Bishop says to the driver, "Hold tight." He turns to Digby and says, "Nice to meet you, Dr. Lange. I'm going to need your left hand please." Bishop uses a handheld sensor to locate the RFID chip under the soft, fleshy part of Digby's skin between the index finger and thumb. He takes a large, syringe-like tool and removes the small, pill-shaped tracking device. He shoots it out the window and it settles in the dust behind them as they drive off, the guards still doing pushups in their rearview mirror.

A celebration is underway at Cold Creek Ranch. The Keepers serve up their own moonshine out of mason jars. A huge bonfire reflects off the many happy faces, including a visiting local Cheyenne tribe, as a bison is roasting on a spit. A fiddle is being played as people laugh and dance drunkenly.

"Underdogs win one today, boys. Yeehaw!" Wabash cheers. A fellow Keeper goads him into singing a Johnny Cash song by playing the opening chords on his guitar. "Alright. Alright," he says and stands on wobbly legs, passing to his left a half-drunk jug of moonshine. "From the great Atlantic ocean to the wide Pacific shore," he croons.

Back at the Lodge, Bishop, Boone, Mountain, and Digby commune in a less-than-celebratory fashion, the air notably somber. Mountain is the first to ask, "So, Doc… What's in the box?"

"It's the one thing that can stop them. I designed

it as a countermeasure, in case the weapon ever got into the wrong hands. Essentially, it's a dissipator. It will piggyback onto their energy source and disrupt the invader frequency by scattering that frequency and returning it back to what occurs in nature. In doing so, the body will no longer recognize it as a threat. But we have to get close enough to the cell tower emitting the frequency. It won't be effective until they turn it on. Our only option is to activate it in real time."

"What's their power source? Bishop asks.

"The Hoover Dam."

Boone whistles. "They're going to hit Vegas."

"Bingo. They intend on targeting the conference of a high level individual with a new fuel cell water energy system with an efficiency that would change the game if it got out. Those in the vicinity of the Luxor Hotel will be taken out as well, including high-level scientists and engineers in attendance. It could mean hundreds of thousands of people if we don't find it in time."

Boone offers, "Anything you need, I know who to call. I've got Vegas wired. You can hide out here 'til it's go time."

A lone Keeper monitors the one Ham radio for all of Cold Creek Ranch, the drone used for their drills on a shelf behind his head. A voice comes in through the airwaves. "WF9JKH, KD2DOG," the voice says.

The Keeper recognizes the shock jock's voice immediately. "Hey, Jack. What's up, buddy?"

"I'm leaving my QTH right now, mobile broadcast station from here on out. Too much heat around since my last broadcast. The scope of our enemy is coming into focus. But the voice of freedom cannot be silenced."

"Over that. Quite a show."

"Right now, I'm looking for a place to land."

"We could always use more patriots."

"Some fresh air sounds nice. So 73, KD2DOG from WF9JKH. I'm clear on your final."

"Ok, thanks for the QSO and I'll see you later. KD2DOG, QSY to the 345 machine."

6. DEN OF EQUITY

Purple and white lights explode as fireworks would across the chasmal ceiling of an abandoned warehouse, hidden among the industrial wasteland of Downtown LA. Floor to ceiling windows are covered by multi-colored blackout curtains. Graffiti covers every inch of exposed wall, with sentiments like, "Fuck the Crones", "Stray Voltage", and "Info Porn". A mash-up of Sting's "Message in a Bottle" fills the space at a lusty level.

"In here, it's our time!" yells a male voice over the music, followed by hearty cheer. Elijah wears an oversized top hat and walks to the center of the room wielding a long, black whip. His outfit is eclectic, reflecting harmonious patchwork, his facial piercing and body tattoos mark him for a life off the grid. The disillusioned trust fund son of a successful Hollywood producer turned Silicon Valley wunderkind, he created a niche as a Hacktivist. In defiance of the privilege he was born into, he found romanticism in fighting for the cause and became good at selling a lifestyle of shenanigans. The circle of young men and woman that forms around him mimic his style and resolve. He makes a proper ringleader for this ragtag group of Rogues, refusing to comply with the Order at every and all cost.

Situated at the DJ booth is Shayla, an emaciated, blue-eyed beauty with a rabbit fur Ushanka perched atop her poorly dyed blonde hair. Her perma-smile is infectious. "We love you, Elijah!" she hollers, raising a hand in the air to the beat of the music she's playing.

Those busy preparing food in the makeshift kitchen stop to join the circle. Elijah welcomes them and signals for Shayla to cut the music. She punches a button and jumps down, taking her place next to him. He takes a deep breath and points to the handlebar moustachioed fellow to his left with a fuchsia scarf tied around his neck. "Go for Malakai!"

"One!" Malakai shouts to the air above their heads.

"Two!" screams the pig-tailed pixie to his left.

On it goes, until they reach the number eighty-eight and one baby; Elijah and Shayla's beautiful two-year-old Baby Maya being looked after by one of the more tender female Rogues.

Elijah turns his head skyward and bellows, "Thank you God for being such a dope creator!" Everyone cheers and laughs as those preparing the scant meal return to the makeshift kitchen to begin service. Rancid vegetables lightly boiled and heavily seasoned, mystery meat that is gray and chewy, but surprisingly tasty. Every Rogue is grateful to get a plate.

After the remnants of dinner have been removed and Baby Maya has been put to bed, the Rogues gather in a round table format for the evening's tradition of Sharing is Caring, started in conjunction with the removal of everyone's handheld devices. It was part of the deal to become a Rogue. In the spirit of the fringe, it became imperative that no one put the group in any danger by carrying into the Den anything that could be traced or tracked. Elijah, the only one with access to the outside world, operates on everyone's behalf, using Anti-forensics on a secured encryption proxy server. The game allows for one chosen person to give him a new topic to research. Elijah, taking time out of his busy schedule to save the world, looks up that topic and shares it with the rest of the group that evening. The others are encouraged to contribute anything else they remember. Then, the others take turns sharing something they remember from past topics. Dependency on the internet created a society slowly bred to forget things. This was the old way of keeping accounts of history and an exercise in keeping their minds sharp.

Most keep journals to write down their thoughts and in doing so, relearned how to think for themselves. As Elijah explained, the act of putting pen to paper has the added benefits of not only opening the neuron pathways to the brain, but it kept them offline and out of danger. "The Order controls most of everyday life, but it cannot control the human spirit."

Elijah presents Kristina's choice, along with a photo. "The monarch butterfly. It was like magic when you saw one because they were known to be good luck. You could sit outside, minding your own business, and one would appear and everything would stop. It's as if you'd hold your breath waiting for it to land closer, closer. You would imagine that day would be the day that one of these beautiful creatures would land on you and flutter its wings slowly, as you studied its brilliant orange-red wings, black veins and white spots along the edges.

"The Monarch exhibited the most highly evolved migration pattern of any known insect. They traveled between 1,200 and 2,800 miles or more from the United States and Canada to central Mexican forests, a marvelous migratory phenomenon. Climate change disrupted the Monarch's annual migration pattern by affecting weather conditions in both wintering grounds and summer breeding grounds. Colder, wetter winters were lethal to these creatures and hotter, drier summers destroyed suitable habitats north. Truly remarkable creatures. Alas no more."

After the game is over, Elijah has pressing business. He holds Council in the area of the massive squat they designated the "war room", sectioned off by canvas hung by rope. A map is pinned to a section of the canvas with markings that show the layout and logistics of a plan, with names attached to certain duties.

This select group of enlightened men and women with nothing to lose listen intently. "Society needs to evolve. Money has controlled how people live for far too long. If there isn't some sort of shift in where the GNP of the country goes, the money that the population generates, then the people are never going to get anywhere with any kind of revolution. It's just never going to happen. Look at the Palestinians. They've been fighting tanks and now drones and planes with sticks and bats and rocks for almost sixty years now. Where is that going to get you if you have all this great revolutionary spirit? It's going to get you nowhere. You've got to get to the Haves who control the resources. The oil companies, the miners for the coal, the electric company, lithium for batteries, lead and dye for paint. If there's ever going to be an effective revolution, we must make allies of the forces that control the resources because only those who control the resources can decide how the population lives."

"Truth!"

"Scarcity is now the norm. Unemployment is rampant and wages are too low. Natural disasters create millions of displaced refugees. Homelessness is an epidemic. The misuse of surveillance has created a different kind of society in which freedom to move unobserved is a privilege only afforded the rich. These manufactured crises allowed the Order to quash our voices in the name bureaucracy based on hypocrisy. Our government gave away our country to authoritative 'experts' who control the very paper our money is printed upon. A fire sale of greed! Everything from the middle down is compromised. People are feeling more stress than ever before with no end in sight. Policies that guarantee impoverishment, dooming us to fail. The people have been screwed by those fucking up this country for too long. But what you allow is what will continue."

"Truth!"

"By sharing resources, sharing the products, automation can work in our favor and not just exist to replace the workforce. With the reallocation of ill-gotten gains, with the amassing of resources, co-operatives can have abundance. The evolutionary self must do better. We must regain compassion. The goal is to transcend and become transcendent. But how do we transcend when we live in a world where everything is about the self? We must embrace the evolutionary self that is fully engaged and confrontational in every way and embrace the life force that it breeds."

"Truth!"

"We have the power to transcend and move forward on a par with the masters of society, to do battle with them on an equal level playing field and protect the character of our country. That's activism. Be brave. For others always. And for yourself, ultimately."

They cheer. He looks at their beautiful, shiny faces and smiles. "Now let's see what's on tomorrow's agenda." He turns to the map and his tone takes a mischievous turn. "We received Intel from the Watchers. Looks like the Haves will be dining out tomorrow."

Enforcer Richie Wick is punching a bag in his garage at night, listening to bad 80's music. An American flag hangs on one wall, a full-length mirror on another. Tucked in a corner is a box of kid's toys. He looks over at it and hits the bag harder. He thinks back to the scene he caused at his kid's second birthday party. His wife's friend really got his goat.

"The Order is taking away all our rights!" he had said.

"It's for your protection. You get brainwashed by the liberal media trying to show you how to think. It's for security and safety and you don't know because you haven't been there, man," Richie had replied.

"Security and safety from what? That's just sound bytes and slogans. Think for yourself. Don't you ever take your uniform off, man?"

He swatted the beer can out of his wife's friend's hand and grabbed him by the throat. A bbq carving fork was within reach and he held it up to the guy's eye.

His little girl had screamed, "Daddy!" and the dog started barking.

Everyone was looking at him in fear. "You don't know what it is to be scared because men like me put it all on the line so you don't have to. You fucking pussy." He put the fork down, but the dog's incessant barking put him over the edge. He kicked it in disgust and walked off. That was the very night his wife took his little girl and left him for good.

He sits on his workout bench and wipes his face with a hand towel, reaches for a mini fridge and opens a cold beer, drinking the whole can down.

The next day, he shows up for work in uniform. Some of the men in the locker room are coming off, a few are showering, one guy is polishing his shoes. A fellow Enforcer, and Richie's only friend, sees him and says, "Hey, how you holding up?"

"I'd be better if …"

An Enforcer fresh out of the Academy interrupts him by shouting, "Safety and Security!", followed by an Enforcer salute; a pounded fist over the heart.

Richie shakes his head. *See where that gets you, kid.*

Del sits at a stoplight and sees a shirtless homeless man, towel wrapped around his waist, lathering himself up with a bar of soap, the bus stop his own private bathroom. He spouts off gibberish about anti-gravity and the tech used for space ships.

Malakai pulls up beside her on his bike and twists his moustache. "I hear it's supposed to rain, Delilah."

"And dogs and cats are living together," Del adds, dryly.

"You dropped something," Malakai says and puts a piece of paper under her windshield. He rides off, weaving thru the traffic. Del reaches over and grabs it before driving off, but not before some asshole honks from behind. She gives him the finger and opens the note. It reads, "Auto Salvage on Pine. 3 pm."

Richie's Humvee is three cars behind her, follow-ing the track patch he stuck under her license plate, watching the exchange. His Mobile Data Terminal displays a picture of Del's face and dossier with the "Do not detain" directive splashed across the screen in red.

The Rogues are in position just outside an over-pass, near the exit ramps. Elijah meticulously clocks the speed of the oncoming vehicles with a laser gun, speaking to the others in place via headset. "Twen-ty-three miles an hour, East to West. Go for breach in forty. Extraction team to follow."

Under the overpass, two Rogues carry out a chunky, beat-up lazy boy into the middle of the road and drop it, stopping the target truck. Elijah springs from his position and hits the truck with an electro-magnetic pulse device, overloading the circuit and un-locking all of the doors.

The second team scurries out with compressed air foam hand held backpack systems. They hit the driver and passenger doors with liquid foam that ex-pands on impact, binding the doors in place.

The third team opens the back doors and they begin loading up trays of food into a van driven by Del coming from the other direction.

Elijah navigates through the honking horns be-hind the hijacked truck in a tailored suit jacket with long tails, addressing the stalled motorists. "Gentlemen and Ladies, a minor delay. A few deep breaths and this too shall pass." He grabs some petit fours from the bounty. "A crumpet for your time. Enjoy! Courtesy of the Haves."

After they load as much food as they can carry, Elijah and the other Rogues jump on their tricked-out Vespas and take the ramp onto the freeway and disappear, Del gunning it behind them.

Outside the House of Blues Gospel Brunch, volunteers are dressing the long line of homeless in Sunday best from bags of donated clothing. Inside the darkened interior, old ladies wear brightly colored jackets and matching skirts, with big hats and shoes to match. They sway to the live music being played onstage, waving their matching kerchiefs in the air. An elderly black lady, wearing head-to-toe canary yellow, fans herself with a program. "Lordy, is it hot in here!"

The Rogues arrive and Elijah makes a grand entrance by climbing on the stage and pronouncing, "Farthings for the Believers. Sustenance for the soul. Blessed day for all!" The ladies clap, with a few "Amens", as the Rogues begin unloading the food from the van in the parking lot. The week-old orange juice and stale muffins on the buffet table are replaced with freshly squeezed juice, salmon platters, Tuscan Truffle egg salad, toasted french croissants, and fancy desserts on silver trays. Elijah bounds over to do the honors of slicing up the prime rib at a carving station. "Don't forget the au jus!"

"Holy Ghost power!" The women eat and dance around on stage to the band, stomping their heels and spinning in circles.

Richie secretly watches the back of the House of Blues from his Humvee parked across the street. When he sees the van emptied, he calls it in.

Enforcers show up on the scene, taking down a few of the Rogues who aren't able to get away in time, Del being one of them. "Only speak if you don't need your face!" an Enforcer shouts into a megaphone.

Richie gets out of his Humvee and pounces. "Back off, boys. Don't get between a hungry man and his meal," he declares, acting the lion to hyenas. He lifts Del from the ground, hands zip-tied, and puts her in the back of his vehicle. "You owe me a meal."

Del returns his stare through the rearview mirror as they drive. "Frat boy beating your chest. You guys get drafted right from the cave."

"You're just a born expert, aren't ya."

"At least I care about my fellow man. You do the Order's bidding all day long. Are you hoping for that big pie in the sky? Or are you content being a slave to the system."

"You group me in with the rest of those guys. That just seems lazy."

"You are what you do."

"It might be what I do, but it's not who I am."

"Mr. Sensitive, I'm sure."

"I have my sensitive parts. I'll draw you a diagram."

Del does her best not to smirk.

Richie pulls up to an Italian restaurant. He helps her out of the Humvee and walks with her to the door. He unhooks her zip tie, playfully fixes her hair and opens the door. "After you."

She shakes her head and walks inside.

The restaurant is busy serving lunch. They are seated at a cozy table in the back. Richie is all smiles.

"You must be very pleased with yourself."

Richie hands her the bread basket. "Carbs?"

"Am I under arrest?"

"Does this look like County?"

"Am I free to go?"

"Not until you've had the tiramisu. Now, THAT would be a crime."

"Ok, Copper."

The waiter takes their order and walks away. "Porterhouse steak. Hooah!"

"Were you in the Army?"

"I saw war."

"What did you see?"

Richie sits back in his chair. "Our purpose was to make things better, to be a part of something greater. But when you hear women and children scream over and over again and you're the cause of it, finding the positive becomes a challenge."

"Why did you go in the first place?"

"Didn't do that great in school. Army recruiter

thought I had potential."

"I'm sure he did. Fresh meat. I mean, look at the size of you."

"First call when I got back was from Enforcer Recruitment. And seeing as how I didn't have a lot of options, I thought I could be useful."

"So, you've just been a blind follower your whole adult life. How's that working out for you?"

"Pretty empty, actually."

"Good news. You're human."

The drinks arriving does nothing to interrupt the intensity of their gaze.

A member of the Amorphous Cell watches coverage of a journalist interviewing a shirtless, sweaty man from his front porch in the deep South. "Thank god. Thank god they found a cure. It's expensive, but thank god. We been prayin' on it."

Bishop, back from Cold Creek Ranch, enters with the Nest's resident lab technician. Everyone stops what they're doing and looks up. Bishop speaks in a hushed tone. "You all know Dr. Phillips." The room nods "Please tell them what you told me."

"We compared the vial containing the vaccine Evomune that Stringer left behind in Delilah's cab to the one that recently went to market for public consumption. The latter tested positive for the HCG antigen. HCG is a chemical developed by the World Health Organization for sterilization purposes, proving this to be a well-coordinated exercise designed to sterilize all those who take it, with only the one dose."

"Damn it!" Leland slams his fist. "So this is their plan? If they don't get us in their first round of viruses they go after our fertility. And they're charging a thousand bucks a shot? Fucking genius."

Amir interjects, "The first stratagem of a conspiracy is disinformation. Remember how they reported heroin overdoses in Skid Row? We're among the very few who know better."

"We've got to get the word out immediately," Bishop says.

"Who's going to believe it? Frankly, it's too diabolical to be believed." Leland remarks.

"I have the perfect conduit. He's one of their own. Leland, I need John ready to launch on the double." Bishop heads to the lab.

The table has been cleared of their lunch dishes, one Tiramisu between them.

"So, what did you want to be when you grew up?"

"You're going to laugh." Richie pushes the plate towards her, making it easier for her to reach.

"Most definitely."

"I wanted to write poetry."

"I hear there's a lot a money in that."

"And why I didn't pursue it."

"I can totally see it. A real tough guy poet. Like

146

Bukowski." She takes a bite and immediately changes her opinion about this sumptuous treat. "Write what you know. Write about the war. I'd read it."

"You're making fun of me."

"While that is my nature, I currently am not."

He swallows the rest of the wine in his glass and closes his eyes. "He's out on the street, and he's probably thinking, why the hell is she so tough? What made her this way? A thoroughbred in the company of nags. Then he's thinking, it's her spirit. It's too powerful. She's a giant. She cannot be contained. She cannot be tamed. Like a wolf or some mad beaver, she's out in the world. Can she slow down long enough to notice that one special guy? Mid glee, the world made sense. Birds made love to other birds, songs crossed the bridge, and all was wonderful in this fantastic world. Where a glorious, mad girl found her heavyweight match. Where people said yes to dessert." He opens his eyes. "The end?"

"Doesn't have to be."

Three minutes before Reilly Williams is supposed to go on, he practices into camera. "Today the Senate voted on allocations for CERT, to arousing applause," he smirks.

The Director confirms sound check. Reilly taps his pencil on the desktop, staring into space. In a low register, he warms up with vocal exercises. "Those old boats don't float."

An intercom summons him. "Reilly Williams, Network President Hersh requests your presence in his office."

"He's in the building? It's been years." He turns to a production assistant. "How do I look? I know, I look great." He exits the studio and makes his way to the President's office.

Reilly Williams remains seated at the anchor desk, arbitrarily tapping his pencil, lost in thought. He appears to be daydreaming.

Reilly knocks on the office door of President Hersh, the media mogul. "Mr. Hersh? You wanted to see me?"

"Please. Call me Humphrey. Have a seat, Reilly." Reilly sits. "You're a very valuable part of this network. You've always had the highest ratings. That is why we've chosen you. Truth is, we have spies among us. You're the only one that we can trust. We know we can count on you because you're the best. Are you up for the challenge? Can you do it?"

"What do you need me to do, sir?"

"When you introduce the vaccination story, read this notecard instead. Go ahead and take it with you. And when you're done, you will be handsomely rewarded by yours truly. Now go on!"

Reilly takes out the earpiece and sets it on the anchor desk. The red light indicating a taping is in progress comes on and the Director says, "And we're live in 3, 2…" He points his index finger at Reilly.

"Ladies and gentlemen, I've been made aware of some very important news, and it's my duty to share it with you. You're being lied to. Stop taking the vaccines. They're sterilizing you. Population control is real."

They cut the camera. He continues, "The war has been declared. No one is safe."

They shut the spotlight off. "What the actual fuck, Reilly. Are you drunk? We're live, for Chrissake," the Director shouts.

"I'm the only one he can trust. You're with them, aren't you."

"Go home. Get the fuck outta here. You're finished." As the Director walks off the set, he calls out, "Somebody get security down here."

Reilly places a call from the back seat of his chauffeured Town Car, trying to reach President Hersh. He gets his secretary on the line. "Please tell Humphrey the mission has been completed."

"Mr. Hersh is on vacation in Aruba with his family until the end of the month."

Reilly returns home to find his broadcast has gone viral on the Darknet. His phone starts to blow up with calls. He shuts it off and pours himself a drink.

Three scotches in, he ambles over to take a shower. A man dressed in black from head-to-toe is waiting behind the bathroom door. As Reilly begins to undress, the man expertly snaps his neck. When his body is found days later with a robe belt tied around his throat, reports of his apparent suicide shook the nation.

7. The Kettle

A cluster of teens are gathered by an abandoned building in a dirty, run-down part of the nation's capital. Weeds and human feces litter the terrain. The teens huff gas out of brown paper bags and entertain themselves by throwing rocks at each other and howling. A lone black boy listening to an outdated iPod pulls a can of spray paint out of his backpack and tags the side of the building with ROGUE FOR LIFE.

An Enforcer Drone flies overhead and the static preceding the forthcoming announcement causing the kids to cringe and start running in all directions. "Cease and desist all activity. Force to be engaged."

The defiant teen eyes it surreptitiously, bends over and picks up a chunk of concrete from the crumbling edifice, hurling it at the predator drone, the loud music in his ears strangling fear.

"Lamar, no! Dude, what are you doing?" a friend calls from over his shoulder, continuing to run.

The chunk connects and bounces off of the drone's steel frame, setting off a high-pitched alarm. Lamar begins to run as the drone follows closely from above, sending a global positioning signal to the nearby Enforcers, who are quick to respond. Tires screech in front of the boy trying to lose the drone in a dark alleyway. He turns to run the way he came and is startled by a loud bang. As he is hurled forward by the searing pain to his chest, his slack jaw cracks on the

151

pavement, the bullet ripping through most of his left lung and arteries. The music fades from his ears as the world falls forever dark.

The cavernous room would be pitch black, if not for the blue-ish white glow of the thousands of monitors neatly lined in seemingly infinite rows. Hard-wired machines and minds, the drone operators focus intently on their twelve-hour duty as preeminent voyeurs, challenged to perform as tirelessly as the all-seeing peeping toms they control.

Pocket stares blankly at his own bird's eye view before him of the body of a dead boy, looking especially small and crushed amidst the piles of refuse lining the alleyway. A single bell alerts the kill and those boys closest to Pocket react with cheers of encouragement in a Cobra Kai-like atmosphere. One yells, "Pocket is stone cold!" Another adds, "Cutting the grass before it grows out of control!" The boys high-five each other like gamers would after placing and then return to their consoles, newly recharged.

Pocket looks down at the controls in his hands and sighs heavily. His unruly hair falls in his face as he discretely takes a slender flask from his combat boot and pours a portion of its contents into the can of coke on his console, unnoticed.

Today, he's just doing his job. The luster has worn off. The pragmatic experience of playing a cog in the wheel of warfare and contributing to the deaths of innocent people through the use of a control panel has left an indelible impression on him.

The break room has a dehydrated, greenish hue to match the atmosphere. An operator is explaining to a new kid, barely sixteen, the origin of the Kettle. "Comes from a group of hawks. Enforcer Drones are eyes in the sky. Through facial recognition and built-in thermal capabilities, the drones can easily tag someone day or night. If we do our jobs right, there's no escape."

The kid seems to like what he's hearing, gung-ho at the thought of wielding such power. "I want to see some punks go down! Blammo!"

Pocket walks into the break room and the operator, upon seeing him, starts bragging. "This mother fucker right here never had to do any work on his evals. Always tested in the pocket, hence his name. Pocket once flew three birds for three months straight! Pocket ain't playin'."

The newb is impressed. "No way!"

"Bullshit. It was actually two planes. The third was my VR shadow." Pocket grabs a protein bar out of a basket on the counter and an energy drink from the communal fridge.

"Doesn't it get hard sometimes?"

Pocket stares at him, bleary-eyed. "Just do your job. Nobody wants to hear any bitching. You want to talk to a therapist about it, you'll lose your security clearance. There's an in-house chaplain that will listen, but he'll just tell you it's god's will." He takes out the flask as the other guys in the break room silently look on. "What whiskey will not cure there is no cure for." He drains the contents down his throat.

Pocket drags his feet all the way home and immediately upon entering, turns on his secure computer to Modern Warcry. He grabs a fresh bottle of Jack from the kitchen and slips on his gaming headset. Drinking straight from the bottle, he washes down an Adderall. He types the necessary code to log into an encrypted group chat and listens in on the current live stream. Jack Hammer has managed to track down Matador and is conducting an interview at an undisclosed location. Pocket sees Freeman1010, aka Elijah, in the chat room and says hi.

Elijah is typing away at his computer in a corner of the Den. The Rogues busy themselves making clothes for each other, taking turns dancing with Baby Maya and teaching her new words in sign language. At two, she is able to create sound but decides it isn't her time to speak yet, so she communicates what she wants through signs. Her community is happy to oblige. They love her and love dressing her in funky clothes, reflected in her itty-bitty Iggy Pop tee-shirt and pink tutu.

Shayla appreciates the love shown her special little girl. As the only parents here, Elijah and Shayla naturally became the Mom and Pop of the Rogue shop, providing the bottom line if ever a disagreement arose, which wasn't often. The healthy cooperative practiced peaceful coexistence.

The Silver Bullet is parked at a campsite on the outskirts of Cold Creek Ranch. Inside is the mess of a man on the run, rife with paranoid gadgetry. An American Flag is draped across the windows, green plastic GI Joes are taped to the dashboard, and a Welcome to Roswell postcard is taped to the controls.

Jack Hammer wears a beret and a shoulder holster. "You know because of your call, I got thrown out of my studio. Too many death threats."

"I'm terribly sorry. That was not my intention," Digby's soft voice is sincere.

"Are you kidding? I'm a patriot. Comfort makes me nervous."

Outside, Mountain and Wabash are on security detail. After racking-up their horses, Mountain sits at a picnic table and lights a cigar, pulling from a flask as he watches Wabash shoot prairie dogs with a homemade blow gun. "Y'all can scurry. Y'all can hide. I'm gonna getcha 'ventually!" Wabash hollers after them.

Jack Hammer continues from inside. "We have to get the word out."

"It's imperative people know the truth. They are going to take a lot of people out and make it look like a natural disaster if we don't do something about it. It's time to expose the vast hidden net that has been cast over the world for control and manipulation, just as the creators of that net begin to use their resources to cull the population. We have to act fast."

Pocket is following the live stream closely, typing a comment on the message board, "Take that, Tyranny!" A thunderous boom causes him to jump in his chair. He turns to see a team of Enforcers bust open his front door and drag him forcibly out of his house. They throw him into the back of an Enforcer Humvee, placing a hood over his head.

The group chat still open, Elijah is awaiting a reply from Pocket, typing, "U there, Skyking777? Are you AFK? U there? U there? U there? U there?" There is no response.

Pocket is driven to a base and thrown onto a military cargo aircraft, two soldiers flanking him, the hood still in place. When they arrive at their destination, it is late at night. They walk him down a long corridor and enter a room, removing the hood. He peers around the nondescript white room, adjusting his eyes, as they strap him to a gurney on his side and in a fetal position, head and body constrained.

Something is wrong, thought Elijah, still fishing for Pocket's whereabouts late into the night. He reaches out to different channels, typing frantically. "Has anyone heard from Skyking777?"

"Looks like Skyking777's a sleeper," types another gamer.

Elijah is unravelling. Pocket is nowhere to be found.

Shayla comes over and gently puts a hand on his shoulder, Baby Maya asleep on her hip. "He'll turn up, babe. Stop worrying."

"It's hard to maintain a positive mind frame when you're in danger of losing everything."

"Well, you haven't lost us. We're standing right here."

"You don't know what these people are capable of, Shay. Pocket never goes MIA. He knows the value of staying connected. It's a security issue. I know they got him. And I'm next."

He pulls away from Shayla and grabs a bottle of booze from the kitchen. He whispers something to a rough-looking Rogue who nods and makes for the door.

Braun walks through the door of the nondescript white room and takes a seat on the chair next to the gurney. "Today is your lucky day. You've put in your time. You've been an excellent operator, highly regarded. Now is zee time to give us zee information vee need. Cooperate and your life vill be spared. You vill live to see another day, isn't zat nice? You can retire verever you vant, full benefits. Pick a place on zee map and vee vill send you zair." He removes a dat recorder from his lab code and sets it down on a nearby table. "You're called Pocket, yah? You're a smart guy,

Pocket. Zis is vut vee are going to do. Vee know you are not zee mastermind behind zis. Vee need to know the extent of zee leak. How many in your organization and vut are zair names?"

"I've seen enough movies to know how this ends. You're going to kill me, regardless. Go fuck yourself."

"Vye choose to make zis more difficult? Vee vill find out zee truth izer vay."

"You don't even realize they're using you. They'll sell you out the first chance they get. You'll never be accepted by them because you're not one of them and you're never going to be one of them. At least we know we're being played."

"Dear boy, you don't appreciate zee elegance of a symphony. I am zee conductor. I bet you wouldn't know a fine wine if it punched you in zee mouth!"

"And I bet you have all your research digitized and the Order has full access to all your files. Am I right? I'm right, aren't I. With a push of a button, you can be replaced. See, you're nothing but a slave, too blind by your own determination to see what's really going on. Do you honestly think they're going to let you join their ranks? Breed with their daughters? The pathetic thing is you still think you matter to them."

Braun remains unphased, sensing this is a waste of his valuable time. "Misguided child, I appreciate your resolve. I vas a boy once, too. Curious by nature. Idealistic. Not like you, of course. I knew my place in zee vurld and knew not to disrespect zee hard vurk of others. Zair is always a reason, you know, why zees sings are done. It's zee bigger picture you're sorely missing."

Braun stands and walks around the gurney to a small instrument table. He takes hold of the ridged handgrip of a steel lumbar puncture needle with a scalpel-type point and a tubular hilt. Feeling with his hands the top of Pocket's pelvis bone, he identifies the correct place and inserts the needle into the fourth and fifth lumbar level of his spine, entering the space where the fluid is contained.

Pocket cringes from the burning sensation.

He returns to his seat, straightens his coat, and clears his throat. "Zee longest ten seconds of your small, leetle, life." He begins counting back from ten.

Pocket's eyes become glassy, the inebriation settling in.

"Now, take me back to zee day you ver brought into Operation Alpha, in an apparent cooperative and organized effort to hack our CAV. Who is Freeman1010?"

A thirteen-year-old Pocket was in his room playing Modern Warcry. His Mom worried that as a first-person shooter game, it would be too violent for her sensitive boy. He told her it's just a game, that it doesn't mean anything. So, she let him play, his online community his only friends. They had a way of speaking to each other that made him feel they lived

159

in a world of their own creation.

"You fragged my 'nade."

"Jacking my kill, bro."

"Zero. KIA"

"Congrats, Bucker! You got an extra 10 points while I'm sitting here on fat 50s because I'm doing real life shit."

"I quickscoped with a kosha because I rule!"

One player stood out from the rest because of his grandstand speeches after winning a round. "The financial divide cannot be sustained," Freeman1010 would say. "The future is going to belong to those who are smart enough and brave enough to challenge the status quo." There would be backlash from the other players, but these messages piqued Pocket's interest. When the day came that Freeman1010 proposed the next step, Pocket bit.

"There's more to this. You know there is. Don't be on the wrong side of history. If you want to know more, find the Advanced Warfare secret cave glitch. Out of map. If you can."

Pocket accepted the challenge. After much searching, he found an undisclosed entryway. The game pixelated as he passed over into an unknown vortex. The game reset the visuals to reveal the dark belly of the cave. The sound of water dripping was almost harrowing, setting his nerves on edge. His machine gun led the way as he explored the tunnels, keeping his trigger finger at the ready in case it was a setup.

He travelled through a dark tunnel and turned a narrow corner. The game opened up to a spacious cave, light pouring in from fissures in the structure above. Tough guy playable characters dressed in army fatigues appeared before him, ready for battle. They wore tactical gear, helmets, war paint, and one sported a Mohawk. They stood gathered together listening to a playable character donning long dreads and a customized strike steel half mask. Freeman1010 was holding court. "If you're here, you're awake. Good for you," he said. "To understand the tiger in the long grass, you have to first know who they are. Big money has corrupted our institutions based on hypocrisy, creating a monumental imbalance of power structures in the modern age. It's no longer conspiracy. It's happening right before our eyes."

"What's our objective?" Mohawk asked.

"Our objective is clear. We are going to turn their tech against them. These powerful dark suits are threatened by Hacktivists who could infiltrate and shut down entire online systems with the click of a button. It's time to neutralize the threat to our very existence. It's a moral imperative we lean into the fight."

"What can I do?" Pocket asked.

"Your level of commitment depends on you. Meet us here next week, two tiers up." Elijah looked around the cave and cried, "Stand up for the Vox Populi!" The others cheered. Pocket joined in.

A fifteen-year-old Pocket competed in a Modern Warcry World Championship Tournament and won. Men in dark suits approached him and recruited him for drone operations. He was taken to a facility where drone pilots groomed young children, enacting drills through 3D high tech video games simulating resistance on enormous consoles. Taking full advantage of the emerging gamer's enhanced skill set, Pocket was handed the controls and tested while the dark suits conferred in the shadows.

He began his sensor-operator course during which airmen instructed him on how to pilot real drones in every condition under every scenario. He excelled on his aptitude tests and went on to train to be an imagery analyst. They told him he had the makings of a hero.

After training, he joined the Kettle, getting a fresh buzz cut to celebrate the occasion. *I thought it was going to be the best thing ever. I couldn't believe my luck. Who gets paid to play video games all day? Well, the excitement didn't last long. The repercussions began to weigh heavily on me when I realized these were real human lives becoming bug splat on the screen. They had turned us into accessories to murder for the Order.*

He could no longer ignore his conscience and began working with Elijah and the Rogues to penetrate the system. A sense of family was created in the shared camaraderie. They even invited him to a party they threw at the Den. Being on opposite coasts, he attended virtually.

Braun interrupts Pocket's stream of consciousness to probe further. "Describe zee Den."

"It's an industrial warehouse converted into a loft space. There are heavy curtains on the windows, all but one. It's a beautiful, blue day outside."

"Look out zee window for me. Vut do you see?"

"A big gold sign with an animal on it."

"Read zee sign out loud for me."

"Spearmint Rhino," he says. Braun writes it down.

Pocket starts speaking gibberish as his brain begins to shut down, signaling the end of the session. Braun stops the dat recorder. The boy is drooling on himself, losing brainstem reflexes in the absence of activity. Braun exits the room, leaving Pocket to die alone in the interrogation room, his head still belted to the bed.

The next morning, Baby Maya wakes Shayla up and signs the word "hungry". Shayla looks over and sees that Elijah is not in bed next to her. She changes the baby and steps out to the main living area to find the Den a mess. Half-dressed men and women are passed out on the beat-up couches, bottles of booze litter the table, remnants of cocaine smear the glass surface.

Elijah's sits at his computer, rocking in place, watching the clock. His mood is raw, exasperated by staying up all night. When it hits 7:00 am, he quickly joins their encrypted chat room and sees that Pocket has not logged in from his work computer. Pocket, from day one, has been one hundred percent reliable in their daily check-ins. He jumps up, grabs his jacket, and heads out without a word, leaving Shayla standing there dumbfounded.

The local seedy bar is open for business and there is a surprising number of people inside at this early hour, belly up. He slides in and asks the bartender if he can use the phone. He gets a hard no. "Please," he begs, finding it hard to hide his anxiety. "Can I give you the number and you can place the call? It's my grandmother. I think I left the oven on in her house and I'm worried the place is gonna blow." He produces a scrap of paper and passes it over to the cranky bartender, his hand shaking. The bartender sizes him up and decides to help him. "Thank you. Her name is Martha."

A fit, sixty-seven-year-old Watcher sits in her small apartment reading a novel, a picture of her son killed in the war framed beside her. The phone rings and Martha answers in a voice suggesting she is much older and frailer. "Oh, dear," she cries. "Let me see about that. Might take me a bit, this darned hip!" She sets the landline phone down, slides into her tennis shoes and sprints out her front door.

The door of Pocket's small house next to her apartment complex is splintered from being kicked in. The house is empty, a vacuum of space where the computer once sat, his personal effects left on the coffee table. She returns to her apartment and picks up her landline phone. "Oh my! The turkey is cooked! Please tell my grandson he took his computer but left his wallet and keys here. The kids today. They're so distracted. I blame the darned internet!"

Elijah's face falls. "Fuck!" He hurries out of the bar.

The Den is just beginning to stir, a combination of electro-house and dubstep already being pumped through their sound system. Elijah storms in and races to his computer, running security measures, deleting files, and erasing his electronic footprint. As fast as he can, he is destroying evidence in droves. "Come on. Come on!" he says to the computer's screen, biting at a thumbnail, manic.

Shayla approaches, wearing her anger like a badge. "What the hell, Elijah? I told you, if this happened one more time, I'm taking the baby and going to go live with my mother. I don't want to live like a college student. This is ridiculous. You're a fucking mess!"

He ignores her, unable to break his locked gaze on the computer screen as years of files are being deleted before his eyes.

Shayla takes Baby Maya and sits over by the window, opening the multicolored blackout curtain to get some air. The baby is in her lap, facing the window, making the sign for "bird". Shayla is calming down, for the baby's sake. "Bird. Good, Maya!" She mirrors the sign and kisses her little girl. The baby continues to make the bird sign. "Do you see a bird, my love? Where is there a bird in this neighborhood." She turns and sees an Enforcer Drone just outside the window, inches from her face. Her scream cuts deep.

Elijah turns and sees the drone. "Shayla! Get down!"

Shayla looks out and sees a dozen drones surrounding the building. Richie Wick and a team of Enforcers flood the streets below, guns drawn. Elijah runs to the window and covers it with the curtain.

Static precedes the drone's computerized announcement. "This dwelling is in violation of Penal Code 459 PC. Come out with your hands up or we'll shoot!"

The Rogues are in full panic mode. "Day May! Day May!" they call out, grabbing their shoes and hats and running towards the rusted caged elevator for hauling furniture back when the warehouse was a function of industry. They start piling into the lift, Shayla and baby Maya behind them. "Elijah! Come on!" she screams.

"I have to wipe this server. I'll meet you down there!" he yells back.

Shayla is filled with fear as they squeeze the old

166

industrial freight cage elevator closed behind them, beautiful Baby Maya calm despite the storm of trouble afoot.

They get to the basement and run down a long alleyway to a back gate. They run through the gate and scatter in all directions. The Enforcers are there to greet them. They open fire.

Elijah hears the gunfire and looks up in horror. He peers out the window and sees Shayla slowly walking towards Richie Wick, carrying bloody swaddling. He slides to the floor, head in hands. Hard-hitting boots on concrete from the stairwell jolt him into action. He makes it to the elevator and opens the metal gate to a dark and haunting shaft. He leaps forward and grabs hold of a cable and climbs his way up into the darkness above, disappearing in the shadows.

Shayla stops in front of Richie Wick. He lowers his weapon at the sight of her. She looks into his eyes and a screech unleashes, presenting a day harder than he's ever imagined. "Whyyy?" The sound is strangled beneath a grief that can only be measured by time and space. Buried inside the darkness of that scream is the loss of his own daughter, carving into his quietly abandoned pain. *More fucked up lies.* He can't look away. He tries to reach his arms forward but they will no longer comply. *This is your world we invaded. This is your world we've killed.* Shayla drops to the hard pavement, hugging Baby Maya's lifeless body tightly to her chest.

Bava walks out and takes a lotus position on a rug atop an elevated platform in front of a small studio audience. He clears his throat and acknowledges those in attendance. "Greetings, dear ones. Welcome to Manisha. A place of compassion. I am grateful to be your guide. I am Bava." The low hum of deep chanting in the background softens his delivery. With a sad smile, he closes his eyes and begins. "Please know, dear listeners, the burden that is our unrest will shift. The psychology of humankind, that which is responsible for distrust in ourselves and disdain for others, will evolve. Succumbing to temptations towards earthly delights are tests. These desires, the intricacy of choice between the path of finding one's higher power or the giving away of one's power over to the darkness, exist to enable one to come to a different conclusion, finding new strength to resolve it. Lifting oneself from the dark places, shining even brighter, leading the way for others to find their way out of the darkness, is part of life's plan. Even in death, the difficult loss of a life can propel another human's forward shift towards healing, that death is not an end but an awakening.

"We are only here temporarily. And that shouldn't frighten or startle anyone. Children are more aware of this, and this is never more clear as when they build sand castles. Very serious work, sandcastles. They can take all day to play, knowing the water, the weather will wash it away, that it is in fact only temporary. The sandcastle they spend all day building will not be here when they return to the beach tomorrow. But that doesn't stop the purity of the act. They don't need to ask where the act will lead. They remain brave in the moment of their joy.

"There is a wave of Crystal children being born of the Indigos, and it is a gift to learn from their wisdom. Indigos lead with integrity and fight for justice. They are warriors for change. Their unique evolution breaks down the old world model of the traditional ways of thinking, to heal the world of fear and famine. Their purpose comes from a place of compassion and truth.

"Crystal children carry an awareness we've not seen before, a shift away from the old energy into the raising of your consciousness in the face of ego to a higher vibrational frequency. The old energy is set in its ways, out for itself in its way of thinking. This new energy will transform the species into a higher consciousness of being. The new energy says anything is possible, that we can manifest an outcome to serve all, to create a new path to help bring peace and prosperity to our planet and all those who inhabit it. They, along with their Indigo parents, are here to steer us away from archaic systems of the old energy grid so that we may not fail as a human civilization. They are here to usher us all into the Intuitive Age on earth."

8. BON VOYAGE

The SS Canaan is docked under the early morning sun just off of the Santa Barbara Harbor. A bastion of wealth and privilege, the crown jewel is finishing its last minute touches, as tender shuttles deliver thousands of delicate pink Juliet roses and fresh island fruit having just arrived in on a private plane.

With a focus on opulence, the ship's grand staircase opens to ornate double stairs with balustrades of crystal medallions. The floating palace is equipped with a hospital, multiple helipads, a full-scale planetarium and 3D cinema, multiple heated infinity pools, three-Michelin-starred restaurants, the biggest wine cellar at sea, a state-of-the-art theatre, and a seven-seat submarine for underwater exploration.

Each villa is regal in its 18th century décor. Grand entry foyers with hand-laid tiles open to 10,000 square feet of unobstructed ocean views, two private verandas, his-and-hers bathrooms steeped in Italian marble mosaics, heated floors, a rainfall shower and a lavish whirlpool tub. Each suite has made-to-order Savoir of England king-sized beds with Egyptian cotton sheets, walk-in closets, private library, spa, fitness room with a dry sauna, solarium, and a 24-hour dedicated butler with a dining room for ten.

Vanessa Rotterdam is making final decisions on the English fine bone China, covered in cobra skin and available in white or rose gold. "Oh, dear. I can't tell which one to choose," she says to the world's top interior designer at her service.

Amschel is making final touches on his art gallery. "The one on the left should just come out a little more, don't you think? It should come out a half an inch. Even the one on the right." Every piece is installed to a precise specification. "About an inch. A bit more. A bit more. A bit more. Let's have a look."

He turns his attention to the furniture. "Can you move this chair? A bit the right." His staff painstakingly maneuvers it into place. After the chair is moved, he says, "Perhaps a table than a chair" He waits for the change to be made. "That's better, don't you think?" His staff overwhelmingly agrees, as always.

Amschel spots a heavy set girl on her way to the suites, linens under one arm. "Are you a part of the additional staff sent in?"

"Indeed I am, sir," she responds.

"Are you a size fourteen?"

"Ten, sir."

"It's going to be very difficult for you to do this job. Our guests lack any interest in looking at someone frumpy." Amschel signals to have her removed. He looks at his Patek Philippe 5004T and scoffs. "Bully!" With a wave of his hand, he walks off to greet his guests.

Members of the Order and a most nefarious coterie of wealthy elite begin to arrive with their families in their personal armadas. Forced to live mostly in isolation, billionaires spare no expense trying to out-wealth each other, amounting to a schoolyard pissing contest over their mega yachts and the flotilla of heavy security surrounding them. Their kind of wealth needs constant tending to, and that includes full staff and accommodations for that staff.

"Mine's bigger than yours!" Evelyn Rockford claims his laurel from the top deck of his gigayacht to another mega yacht nearby.

"Ugh. Billionaires." Amschel groans, watching the acquired situational narcissism of the ultra-rich as they show off their ego-boosting phallic symbols.

The guests and their children arrive by tenders with Amschel and Vanessa there to greet them. Champagne and caviar are being passed around as staff members discretely haul luggage and racks of designer clothes to their suites.

Amschel cannot control his eye-rolling. He speaks under his breath. "He must have married his sister. It would explain the children."

Vanessa hides her laughter, enjoying her husband for the moment. It reminds her of when they used to have fun together, even if it is at someone else's expense.

Richie Wick pulls up to Del's house unannounced, awkwardly parking his Enforcer Humvee diagonally on her front lawn. He grabs a small, white paper bag from the front seat and heads for the front door.

Del hears the knock and peers outside the front window, hidden by thick drapes. "Mom, it's that fucking cop. What the fuck is he doing here?"

Her mother joins her at the front window. "Ooh, you didn't tell me he was so handsome. There's something about a man in uniform. Honey, answer the door!"

Del opens the door and steps outside. "What now? You tired of being a meter maid?"

He hands her the bag. "Today, I'm a delivery boy. I was stopped at a red light. And I saw an Italian bakery I liked as a kid. This is for you. Tiramisu."

She takes the bag. "Thanks."

"I've had a rough couple of days. Something happened at work and they've given me some time off. I was hoping maybe we could… I thought maybe you could use a break from this godforsaken city and might want to go on an adventure with me?"

"Oh yeah? Where to?"

"I was thinking Vegas. Is that too tacky?"

"Yes. Vegas is too tacky. They even have it written on their sign. Welcome to the tackiest place on Earth."

"Well, I don't mind tacky if you don't mind tacky. Whaddya say?"

"Now?"

"Yeah. If we want to beat traffic."

Del doesn't respond. She turns around and goes

174

inside the house, shutting the door in his face. Her mother is still perched at the front window. "You should go, mija," she says, eyes on Richie.

"Mama!"

"He seems sweet. You work all the time and you need a break. It looks like he needs a break, too. Don't worry, I've got Bodhi. Go have fun. Dance."

"Really?"

"Not all Enforcers are the same. Change is an inside job. Waking up one Enforcer is like waking up a thousand regular civilians." Valentina radiates eternal inner beauty. "You're not the first to entertain romance with a warrior."

Connie, the beautiful, Asian junior analyst posted near Amir's station at the IGA, slowly approaches. *There's something about him I can't put my finger on*, she thinks. Perhaps it's because he doesn't notice her. Connie's beauty is accustomed to beating men off with a stick.

Amir's head is buried in his computer, researching cell towers near and around the Luxor Hotel in Vegas.

"Going on Vacation?" Connie asks a little too close to his ear, startling him and derailing his focus.

Amir glances over his shoulder. "Not exactly."

"What about tonight. Got any plans? It's Friday night. You know what they say about all work and no play..."

He rebuffs her advances. "Not now, Connie."

"Ok, fine," she says curtly and reluctantly returns to her post.

Braun is in the Control Room at Paradigm Solutions, a NASA-like war room with wall-to-wall monitors and rows of German engineers in their positions at their computer panels, wearing headsets and taking readings. They have the strictest orders to report all results directly to Braun, who slowly walks the length of the rows of machines, observing. They are preparing for the night's test run of the Sound of God Weapon, the monitors showing live feed of hundreds of slot machines and their human counterparts, incessantly feeding the one-armed bandits with no signs of stopping any time soon.

The guests of the SS Canaan are enjoying an elegant fifteen-course dinner in the Pavillion Grand. The wives are dressed in top designer gowns, the men in tuxedos.

An eighty-foot screen lowers behind the stage of the giant theatre and a video presentation begins to play as they dine. The video opens to a shot of Earth from outer space. Words appear on the screen. "Where will you go in the pandemonium?" followed by the words, "How will you survive the chaos?" An incoming meteor is shown crashing down on the planet, followed by shots of the Golden Gate bridge with a blackened sky behind it, the tumultuous sea below. Images of military formations, soldiers marching while holding automatic weapons. Bombs fly through the air, riots in the streets confronted by hostile Enforcers. A high-tech logo appears, signifying Canaan. More words appear on the screen. "The Finest in Comfort and Security". The video introduces other Canaans around the world: utopian retreats in Alberta, Gstaad - with images of people skiing under the words "It's your winter home", British Columbia, Argentina, Australia – with images of people golfing under the words "It's your summer home", and Sochi.

The narrator continues, "Bunkers strategically located deep within a limestone mountain." Zooming in from a satellite image of the territory to a close up on the mountain, with images of beautiful countryside. "The world's most elite shelters on Earth are now being prepared, just for you." The words "Impenetrable Blast Doors" and "Modern infrastructure" are superimposed over pictures of the pristine entry tunnels, elaborate living quarters, restaurants, entertainment facilities, and storage. The words, "Your membership is all-inclusive. Canaan. Secured Living."

"So, this is Mezcal. Wow. Tastes like I fell face first into a campfire."

"People love it or hate it."

Del and Richie are bellied up to a semi-swanky

bar. He slides the glass to her. "All yours, pretty lady," he says, taking in her red dress again with a whistle. He asks the bartender for a Jack and Coke. "It was a pretty easy transition. I mean, I didn't have much education before I went into the Army. When I got home, I had a pamphlet with my name on it from the Enforcers Academy saying that I had been preapproved. They even gave me a credit line."

"Don't you find it hard to be mean to people all day?"

"It's just a job. But, I mean, yeah. Increasingly more so. You feel like… at some point you know how everything's going to play out. Family, job, and the day to day of it wears on you. I know it wore on her."

"This is your wife you're talking about."

"Yeah, I wasn't exactly a good partner."

"You think you know how your life is going to turn out. It never looks like how you imagined."

"It's never simple."

"Why can't it be simple? Why can't life be simple?" They both laugh and drink. "To the simple life!"

After the video presentation ends, Amschel gets up on stage to speak. "When you consider that 1959 was a time when the likes of Dean Martin, Frank Sinatra, and Marilyn Monroe were everywhere, then you know what it is to have aged well. We are extremely lucky to have the only three-hundred and six bottles of Dom Pérignon Rosé Vintage 1959 ever produced and never officially sold. Well, the Shah of Iran was able to sneak in a few bottles."

The audience laughs haughtily as stewards begin pouring glasses of the impossibly expensive bubbly.

Amschel takes his seat as the entertainment portion of the evening begins. A holograph taken from the live show hosted by Johnny Carson illuminates the stage. The Rat Pack sings for them, accompanied by a full orchestra, and as the antics of their performance unfolds, the guests howl with laughter.

Del and Richie return to their hotel room at the Mandalay Bay Resort and Del immediately heads to her overnight bag for an Advil.

"You ok?" Richie closes the door softly.

"I just can't shake it. I have this ringing in my ears, like some sort of alarm going off. It's a gnawing feeling, like I just went to a loud rock concert or something. My head is splitting."

"You know, now that you mention it, I've been kinda feeling it, too. I thought it was the Mezcal. I was hoping you'd just roofied me."

She slips into bed. "Do you mind if we lay down? I'm really not feeling well."

"Let me get a cool washcloth. Can I get you a ginger ale or something?"

"No, that's alright. You don't have to."

"Hold on. There has to be something in this

minibar here. Let's see." He opens the tiny fridge and rummages through its contents. "What the fuck is a LaCroix?"

"It's trendy soda water. Yeah, I'll take one of those."

He walks it over. "Do you want ice?"

She takes the cold can and rests it on her temples.

"Can I get you a sandwich?" he asks.

"I'd love it if you'd lay down next to me and put your arms around me. That's all I want right now," she says. "And no boners."

He gets into the bed with her, still clothed, and wraps his arms around her. "You know, I could power through it. I could fight my way through it, if I had to."

"What?"

"I'm just saying, if you wanted to, I could tough it out for you."

"As sweet as that offer may be, I really can't move my head right now. I just want to lay still."

"I'm just telling you, if I had to take one for the team, I could do it."

"You're a hero."

Mills wanders the halls of the underground facility at night, feeling like a caged animal. He sees the slightly ajar door of Bishop's empty office, an open laptop sitting on his desk. He pushes the door open and takes a seat in front of it. A folder labeled "Banking Cartel" catches his eye. He clicks on the icon and finds documents stemming back over a hundred years on how the Rotterdam family has perpetrated the greatest crime in modern history. Mills reads aloud. "The Federal Reserve, a private company that is neither Federal nor a Reserve, forces its citizens to pay taxes to them every time they get a paycheck, profits that exceed $150 billion per year. The most gigantic trust on earth and the invisible government by the power of money.

"Under the Patriarch, heads of every industrial empire in the world and international banksters formed the Council on International Affairs, the promotional arm of the Order, to divide the masses through political, economic, social, and religious means. Their tax-free foundations provide the capital needed to support their constituents in the media, academics, and nearly every elected office in America. They have ties to arms deals, drug smuggling, child sex rings, and 'suicides' of those who get too close to the truth. They are not associated with the government. They *are* the government.

"The Order's agenda to cull the population appears to be in place through coordinated conflicts: toxic substances injected into the air and water, Genetically Modified Organisms in food supplies, promoting the use of drugs with coal tar derivatives while degrading preventive medicine, bioengineered pathogens, and antifertility compounds introduced via vaccines…"

Throughout the night, the members of the Amorphous Cell are honing in on social media chatter coming out of Vegas, following reports of headaches, nausea and nosebleeds. The media shows footage of people in the area doubled over and vomiting in the streets, holding their heads with tear-soaked faces. A reporter on the scene is interviewing a woman in the lobby of a hotel. "We would've had a great time, but the headaches we all got were unreal." A man passing through sees the camera and interjects. "What happens in Vegas stays in Vegas? Good! You can keep that migraine!" he says and storms off, struggling with his luggage.

Reilly Williams's replacement is a young, blonde anchorwoman named Lori Thomas and her high voice is as obnoxious as her world views. "Does everyone in Vegas have a hangover? Wouldn't be too much of a stretch for degenerates. However, it turns out the company who supplied Freon for the air conditioning units to several Las Vegas casinos had a chemical spill at their factory that got into a batch. No word yet on how long the tinnitus will last. Perhaps it's time to do the only thing you should do when you get down on your knees and that's pray."

The Keeper in charge of the Ham radio gets

word from the Amorphous Cell regarding the test run in Vegas. He scrambles out of his shack to deliver the message.

Digby, honing the countermeasure in his room, is interrupted by Mountain. "We got a message from the Nest. Two narrow ladders. The first is twenty feet, the second forty. You have to get out of there by sunset or you'll be blinded by the lights. Once they switch on, the temperatures have been measured at five-hundred degrees."

"I've read that moths are immediately drawn to it, which attracts bats, which attracts owls. It's a whole food chain up there."

"This is happening. Are you ready?"

Digby closes up his case and quietly nods.

The Silver Bullet is gassed up and ready to go, albeit a considerable mess. Jack Hammer, looking a bit scruffy, is clearing out trash under the moonlight to make room for Digby, who is standing quietly clutching his case. Mountain and Wabash, heavily armed, share a look. "We're coming with you. For protection," Mountain says.

"Well, ok then. Hop in. And don't you worry, they can't track us." Jack Hammer boasts, "I got these guys from Bulgaria to cover this beauty head to toe in titanium. It's impenetrable. I'm not paranoid, just risk sensitive." He takes his seat behind the wheel and starts up the engine. "Gentlemen, it's our civic duty to deliver freedom from oppressive forces. Whatever happens, our efforts alone will be met with benefit for all mankind, by the doing. Inaction is complicity."

Balancing on radio equipment and dirty laundry, Mountain states, "Fuck those bastards. We're bringing the fight, boys!"

Topp App's notorious Church Televangelist Sid Fiddler wears a pressed white suit and stands on a tiered stage in front of a room full of his followers. His family is seated behind him at a long table, saucer-eyed men and heavily made-up women hanging on to his every word.

"It's much closer to the end than we thought, folks. The holy sun has risen upon the sodomites. God smite the sinners! Gomorrha will get what it deserves. Choose not to sodomize and gamble away your family's money. Now is the time. Because when you are on God's side, you are always on the right side."

"Preach it!" his followers say in unison from the benches, waving their hands in the air.

"I have something exciting for you, folks. What we have here are twenty-year shelf life buckets of food." He gestures towards the hard to miss wall of white, plastic buckets piled up next to him. "Great for the end of times. You can make tables out of them. You can use them for human waste. And they float! They're just great." He stirs a plastic bucket at his feet of what looks to be creamed corn. "Now, I know your social security checks don't cover the cost of living. You could buy these buckets and eat every day. Just look at those chunks!" He takes a taste and chokes it down. "God, that's delicious. It's so filling and full of flavor." He sets down the ladle and grows emotional, his face contorting into weird shapes. "This has always been my calling. To get people prepared. Because we are in the last days and the Lord is coming with fire. The cows have fallen ill. The chickens have sprung the roost. You have to get prepared because you have no idea what tomorrow will bring. The desperate end of everything you've ever known. It's absolutely vital that you be ready."

9. Omega

A soiree is underway on the deck of the SS Canaan. Chefs spend the day preparing to serve roast suckling pig, carved meats, lobster, and tables filled with mouth-watering desserts. Wives wearing heavy jewelry with their bathing suits are socializing by a faux beach pool on comfortable sun chairs, the gleaming white sand consisting of pulverized marble. A dedicated steward in a tie and cream-colored tuxedo jacket caters to their every need.

"She ripped out a very fashionable Provence style rugged country kitchen and installed enough stainless steel you could disembowel a corpse in there," says a rail-thin wife of a hedge funder with no emotion to her voice. The Teacup Pomeranian in a lilac cashmere onesie does nothing to distract from the extensive plastic surgery that has ravaged her face over the years, amplified by the light of day.

The steward carries over a tray of a frosty, pink liquid served in martini glasses and a plate of Prosciutto Burrata with arugula, Fuyu persimmon, and pomegranate seeds that no one touches.

"Dear," one wife says to the steward, "I know a wonderful orthodontist. Maybe he could help you with those teeth."

"Yes, Madame. Thank you, Madame," he says with a slight bow. His white-gloved hand collects the previous martini glasses, freshly emptied.

"Oh look, there goes Melissa," another wife says with a point of her long, bejeweled finger. "She's already given half of their fortune away. Who does she think she is? Mother Teresa, trying to secure her place in Heaven? And to Africa, of all places! Have you ever been to Africa? Insufferable. I made it a week before I faked an illness so I could return home."

"Anything to distract her from having sex with that husband of hers. You can always tell new money because they're both ugly." The women cackle.

Vanessa winces. *Oh, to be anywhere else but here*, she thinks to herself.

Evelyn Rockford stumbles out, his belly hanging over a powder blue Speedo bikini. He is dancing to a song in his head, already very drunk for the early morning hour. He stuffs bacon and shrimp into his mouth from his oversized Bloody Mary, spilling most of it on the deck. "Pardon me, ladies. Is the hen house full?" he says in his thick, Southern drawl.

His wife is the exaggeration of a Southern Belle, caked on makeup and hair as high as the sky. "Oh, my Lawd, Evelyn. Aren't you a sight! He's such a pill, idn't he? But, he's mah pill. Come here, sugar!" Evelyn saunters over and they exchange Eskimo kisses with the tips of their noses.

One wife is glaring at them. Evelyn shoots back. "Well, whatchu lookin' at, Gwendolyn? I could write a check for yer asshole right now. I could buy it over here and sell it over thar."

An impeccably dressed Amschel approaches. "This reeks of effort," he affronts with the look of someone who has smelled rot. "Evelyn, you boiled owl. It appears you left your shame on the dock. We've got a meeting in the Grand Havana Room in one hour."

Blackwell sits in a white gazebo attached to the pool in white linen pants and a green pastel colored button up shirt, scotch in hand. A gigantic water slide empties nearby and when she resurfaces and climbs out of the pool, he sniffs in Winnie Rotterdam's direction. "My father told me if I ever met a girl in a bikini like yours, I must look her straight in the eyes."

She stares blankly at him and runs off towards her siblings, who are busy teasing the portly son of a billionaire science denier. "Mummy, did you see the submarine? We'll have to get one immediately!"

"Well, you'll never fly in it because you're too fat to be an astronaut." Laughton and Annesley burst out laughing. She pulls out a bottle of Domaine Leroy Chambertin Grand Cru from her leather satchel. Laughton grabs the bottle. "Ahhh, nice. Napoleon was known to drink Chambertin wine," Laughton says, inspecting the bottle. "Not the swill you get from the 1990 vintage, however." He hands it back to her.

She removes a small eye dropper bottle from her pocket and gives her brother a mischievous look. She unscrews the top, fills the tube of the dropper, removes the already uncorked bottle of red, and empties the contents of the dropper into the bottle. "Let's fuck some brats up."

"Oooh, I like your style. What is it this time?"

"Pure MDMA. They won't know what hit them." She turns to the nearest kid. "Hey, you want to try some wine?"

"I've had wine already. What do you think, my parents are poor?"

"Well, then. Here you go, big man." They hand him the bottle and he takes a huge gulp. He spills red liquid all over his face, causing Laughton and Annesley to double over with laughter. "Whoa, look at you! I think I see a hair growing on that chest!"

The kid wipes his face and hands the bottle to Winnie, innocently looking on. She lifts the bottle up to her lips, closes her eyes, and drinks.

Del, wearing a wide-brimmed hat, large sunglasses, and a peach-colored sarong tied at the waist of her bathing suit, sits back on her pool lounge chair, eyes squeezed shut.

Richie appears with two fresh margaritas. "A little hair the dog?"

"Oof. Viva Las Vegas." She takes a large gulp and sets it down on the table next to her chair.

He takes the seat next to her, watching the partygoers frolicking in the pool, some dancing to the music being pumped through the surrounding speakers.

"Thank you for taking care of me last night."

He reaches over and takes her hand in his. "No, thank you. I haven't felt this good in a long time." They sit quietly for a moment. He takes in her beauty, serenely removed from their surroundings. He clears his throat. "The Queen of the desert, her empire is cheese. The booze flows, the music plays, she rises above the sleaze."

She tries not to laugh and says, "Now what will the Queen be having for lunch."

A couple seated next to them are talking about a Vanguard Conference happening at the hotel next door. Del overhears a name she recognizes. "Excuse me. Did you say Arrow Finch is in town?"

"He is," the woman of the duo says, "to show off a new technology they say will put the oil companies out of business. It's happening at the Luxor this afternoon."

Del turns to Richie with childlike enthusiasm. "They're calling him a modern-day Thomas Edison. The man is my son's personal hero. Bodhi would want me to go."

"I thought we'd…"

"As the Queen, I must insist."

The twelve power men of the Order gather in the Grand Havana Room, the Saturday afternoon sun blocked by blackout blinds. A large credenza opens electronically to present multiple wall-mount screens from floor to ceiling.

Amschel comes forward and addresses the men seated in purple and gold chairs, highball glasses in hand. "Gentlemen, today we present a window into the future of our struggle. We begin to defend the inequities of this planet first as a trickle, then as a flood. I present to you Dr. Braun and his Omega Protocol."

One screen becomes live to Braun in the Control Room at Paradigm Solutions. "Esteemed guests, fellow defenders of zee New World. Velcome to a real vorld laboratory. Here, vee are harnessing an energy field like nothing seen before. And zee scope of its power is vast. I admire your hopeful resolution not to yield, zee unshakeable vorth of noble effort vatever zee outcome. Zee gradual theory of zee need for natural selection asserts fundamental aspects of our rational, inventive and ethical activity, justifies zee intricate and vital hierarchy of society, and exemplifies zee idea of perfection vithout restricting zee fundamental significance in vich perfection is aptly perceived as zee pinnacle."

Amschel jests, "The fertile imagination of a scientist." The others laugh haughtily. "Braun, get to it already."

Braun clears his throat. "Vee begin vith Sin City. Las Vegas."

Evelyn interrupts. "The most elaborate strip mall in the world. A perfect target. Sort of a biblical ending, don't you think?"

"Quite so." Amschel offers a tight-lipped smile.

Digby and the others arrive at the Luxor Hotel. On his way out of the Silver Bullet, Jack Hammer takes out his Dirty Harry .44 Magnum pistol from underneath the seat and tucks it into his pants. They all head towards the hotel, Digby clutching his case tightly in his arms.

Mountain points Wabash towards the glass doors of the lobby. "Hang back. I need eyes on the front. If you see any Enforcers, light it up."

"Giddyup."

The top floor takes an eternity to get to. Following the sign to the Sky Beam, Digby turns and says somberly, "If I'm not able to stop them, one of you needs to get Arrow Finch out of range. He's too important to future generations."

"I'll go." Jack Hammer offers. "I've never met a man who can say no to a .44." He gives the men a determined look and without saying any good-byes, he hurries off towards the hotel's Convention Center.

Covered from behind by Mountain, Digby takes the two narrow ladders up to the lamp room at the top of the pyramid, the highest point in the hotel. He hides undetected behind a large, metal air vent and acts quickly.

Del and Richie have changed into day wear and stroll next door to the Luxor. As they approach the entrance to the Convention Center, a large guard in a suit stops them.

"Without the proper credentials, I can't let you in. I'm sorry, Ma'am."

"Damn it!" Del can't hide her disappointment.

"Hey, you can tell Bodhi you were in the same building with Finch. He'll still get a kick out of that. Let's go gamble, whaddya say?"

She allows him to take her hand. They head towards the hotel's casino.

Braun is pacing the tiled floors of the Control Room, doing a system pre-check, communicating with his team. They are checking the major system components.

"Power output feed?"

"Online."

"Transfer signal integrity?

"100 percent."

"Cell tower interference?"

"Suppressing now… Fully suppressed."

A security monitor displays the main generator room of the Hoover Dam, another provides coverage of the people in the casino at the slot machines. "Nutzlose Esser," Braun mutters to himself.

"Sir?" says a nearby technician.

"Oh right, you don't speak German. Useless eaters." He pushes a button on a console. "Here my tigers, some inspiration." The German punk rock song

Sonne by Rammstein is piped in through the loud-speaker. Braun waves his hands in the air as though he were conducting a symphony.

When the song has ended, he gives his subordinates the order to initiate the Sound of God Weapon. The monitor zeroes in on the cell tower nearest the Luxor Hotel. The countdown begins. A woman's calm voice is heard over the loudspeaker. "Five minutes to impact."

The Vanguard Conference in the Luxor's Convention Center begins. Scientists, engineers, and a plethora of media are there creating a buzz in the air.

Self-made billionaire Arrow Finch steps out to the roar of applause. He is a good-looking, young man with a dynamic presence. He begins to speak and the room instantly becomes silent. "One constant in the world of globalization is the growing need for energy. As the landscape grows, so does our need to reduce consumption of carbon-emitting fossil fuels. If we don't evolve fast enough and stall the effects of climate change now, there will be dire consequences for the next generation. We're talking children and young adults already living among us. The question is, what can we do today to make the kind of difference we need?"

The wall behind him slides open to reveal a shiny, red vehicle. "Behold the water-powered car. Energy is produced by splitting water into hydrogen and oxygen using electrolysis, and then burning the gases in the engine with a minimal electric current of barely 0.5 amperes The exhaust of water-powered vehicles consists of water vapor, making it entirely eco-friendly, reducing our fossil fuel use by 85%, a giant leap towards saving the planet. And this generator can be fixed to any gas or diesel engine, depending on their cylinder capacity. We at Vanguard are excited to announce we've finished production on facilities across the country to carry out the conversion from fuel-powered engines to water-powered ones to anyone who wants it, free of charge!"

Applause erupts. A beautiful woman walks onstage carrying a jug of water. She hands it to Finch, waves to the crowd and walks off. Finch takes a drink from the jug and smiles, opens the tank, fills it with water, gets in, and revs up the engine. Everyone cheers. The camera flashes from the media crew are blinding.

Jack Hammer appears at a door to the left of the stage. He speaks to the security guard posted there and mentions the name Turner Boone. The guard radios his superior, gets the authorization, and lets him through. He crosses the stage to where Finch is seated in the shiny, red car. "Sir, your life is in danger. Please come with me."

"What are you talking about? I'm in the middle of a presentation."

"Everything will be explained later. There's no time." Jack Hammer reveals the .44 that's concealed in his waist, under his shirt.

Finch exits the vehicle and turns to the audience. "Please enjoy the refreshments and I'll be back to take questions in just a bit." He follows Jack Hammer off-stage and out through a side door.

Over the loudspeaker in the Control Room, the calm, computerized voice continues the countdown. "Two minutes to impact."

Harlan Braun and his team watch with anticipation.

"Double Down!" Del hollers, crushing it at the Blackjack table as Richie sits back admiring her skill. He looks for a waitress to refresh their drinks and notices a shady looking guy standing by the exit, staring at them.

"What's this now?"

Del follows his gaze and recognizes Wabash. "Hey, I think I know that guy."

Wabash waves her over.

"It appears he knows you, too."

Del scoops up her chips and walks over to him, passing the rows and rows of slot machines. Richie is close behind her.

"You're a friend of my father's, correct? From that ranch? It's been a while, but you have one of those faces."

"Hey Delilah, you have to get out of this building

right now," Wabash rasps, looking around nervously.

"Dude, what's your deal, man," Richie gets in Wabash's face.

"I don't know who your friend is, Delilah, but you really gotta get outta here!"

"Or what, tough guy." Richie shoves him.

"You. Don't. Want. This." Something in Wabash's voice assures Richie that that's true.

"Ok, boys. You both pee really far. Enough."

"Something major is about to go down. An attack."

"What kind of attack?"

"We don't know. But we're at DEFCON 1. Get your girl and get out of here. Do it now, man!"

Something in his urgency sets Richie into motion. He picks Del up, throws her over his shoulder, and kicks the front doors open. He runs towards the lot he parked his Humvee in and when he gets to it, he puts her down and unlocks her door.

"Was that entirely necessary? I have two perfectly functioning legs."

Their eyes lock when they hear a low, dull hum filling the sky. A stranger nearby carrying an oversized plastic cocktail with a funny straw looks suddenly very lost. "Hey, do you guys hear that? What's that sound?" A steady swarm of birds gathers in clusters and flies away from the strip, squawking as they go.

"Is it an earthquake?" Del asks.

"Don't know. Get in." Richie's tone means business. She climbs in.

The multiple screens of the Grand Havana Room, wake to live feed from security cameras in the Luxor and the surrounding areas. Members of the Order wait with certain exhilaration as rows of one-armed bandits devour coin after coin from the cups of poor grannies and overfed consumers. As the weapon is initiated, people fall to the floor, grabbing their heads in pain. The Order watches, desensitized to the snuff-film-like quality.

Braun narrates from the screen projecting the Control Room at Paradigm Solutions, talking directly into camera. "So you see, zee subjects zey are experiencing mild nausea, zey have a powerful ringing in zee ear. Vith zee increased frequency, zee synaptic neurons are scrambled like zey are in a microwave and one thing leads to another and boom! Night night. No more slot machine for you, fatty."

Blackwell's interior jacket pocket vibrates. He walks to the back of the room to take the call.

"The target has resurfaced."

"Send coordinates." He hangs up and makes another call. "I need your services. Sending you the coordinates now." He hangs up, a look of concern growing across his face.

As the Sound of God Weapon makes its way through the crowds, bringing thousands down with it, members of the Order congratulate Amschel on his contribution to the Cull.

"How much ground can this cover? How far reaching is this in a big city?" the Indian business magnate asks.

"I believe it depends on the power source. Braun?"

"Zat is correct, sir. Vee can harness as much power as vee need and zee application is limitless."

"How would you like us to spin it?" asks President Hersh, the media mogul.

Amschel revels in answering. "Well, sun flares, of course. We're delighting in the global warming movement. We can use it to help explain a lot. As Mark Twain put it so eloquently, it's easier to fool people than to convince them they've been fooled."

Jack Hammer and Finch race around the side of the ominous pyramid to find Wabash waiting for them, alone. "Where is he?" Jack cries over the ominous hum in the air.

"No sign yet." Wabash has eyes trained on the hotel exits, hands fidgeting. "I should go in."

"You'll never make it out. Don't you worry. They're coming!" Jack Hammer leads Finch to the Silver Bullet and climbs into the driver seat, pounding a fist on the steering wheel.

Taking full advantage of his Enforcer Humvee, Richie runs red lights, driving up on sidewalks to navigate through the traffic. Emergency vehicles are heading towards the Strip as he and Del drive away from it.

Del frantically scrambles through her purse looking for her phone.

John is still perched in front of Bishop's laptop, bleary-eyed and exhausted. He hears a phone ringing from inside the desk. He locates it and sees Del's name on the incoming call and answers it. "Dad! Something bad is happening. We just barely got out of Vegas!"

"Who's we?"

"John?"

"Yeah."

"That doesn't matter. Where's my father? We're on our way to the Nest now."

Mills jumps up, phone in hand, and runs towards the main headquarters. The panel of monitors project the CCTV cameras from inside the casino. Bishop and the Amorphous Cell watch in horror as people are falling to the floor screaming, holding their heads in pain. "Leland! I need to go in!" he calls out.

"Not now, Milly!"

Still on the phone with Del, he says, "The Patriarch is the source. I have to go under."

"What? No, John. Not without Leland!"

"While he remains alive, they will continue to hijack the system. I've seen what these people are truly capable of. They are the worst of mankind. I have to do it for Bodhi. He deserves the best future we can give him." Mills leaves the main headquarters and heads for the lab. "I'm going to finally put a stop to this madness. Someone has to."

"John, you can't do it alone."

"I wish I didn't know any of this. I wish I could wake up tomorrow and do something ordinary like take Bodhi to a ball game and we wouldn't have all of this suffering at the hands of madmen."

"Please. It's too dangerous. Wait for Leland."

"Time's up," Mills says and hangs up the phone. He enters the lab and hooks himself up to the heart monitor, starting the metronome. His eyes dart as he searches for the target in his mind. He closes his eyes and goes under.

Del stares at her phone, visibly upset.

Richie takes notice. Not sure what to say, he focuses on the road ahead.

Del begins pulling up footage from the Fair Play App of cell phone videos taken from inside the casino. The footage is shocking. People are running in all directions, trampling each other. She cannot contain her tears.

Digby works steadfastly hidden in the shadows of the lamp room, holding his head in pain. The black case lights up as he hones in on the exact frequency necessary to disrupt the invader signal.

Mountain is holding his position at the bottom of the ladders, eyes squeezed shut, staving off the pressure from inside of his skull.

A panel of lights from the interior of Digby's case flash from yellow to green, confirming the signal has been restored to a naturally occurring pattern. "There it is!" he cries, feeling the pain in his head abate instantly. He breathes a sigh of relief.

Members of the Order watch stone-faced, calmly sipping their brandy, unaffected by people screaming in pain on multiple screens. Then, as quickly as it began, the chaos slows to a stop. People pick themselves up, shaking their heads as they help others to stand. Cocktail waitresses hand out bottled water as EMT rushes in to attend to those more fragile to the effects.

"Is this intermission?" Evelyn drawls. "Boy, get me a mint julep," he says to a steward passing through. "I can't wait to see how it ends."

One the screen projecting the Control Room at Paradigm Solutions, Braun is cross-checking the equipment in a frenzy. Amschel turns up the volume on the screen. "Zey reversed zee polarity. Affenarsch! Stand down! Vee have to revamp all zee intake. No, hold, on. Zere ees an alternate field coming from somewhere. Zis is unacceptable!" he screams to his subordinates. "At least give me power on zee back end. Damn it! You fucking toad." The subordinate says something inaudible. "No, I know how it verks. I designed it! It's not supposed to verk zat way. Are vee debating? You fuck!" Braun has his back to the camera, unaware Amschel and the Order are listening in.

Amschel turns away from the screen. "Nothing more malapropos than an emotional scientist," he says, cutting off the transmission. He turns to Blackwell. "This lands on you, B.D. You made assurances."

"On it. Change nothing." Blackwell storms out. Within minutes, he's airborne from atop the bridge.

Digby and Mountain hurry across the parking lot, shaking the ringing out of their heads. As they approach the Silver Bullet, a lone shot is fired.

They climb into the back with Wabash and Finch, Jack Hammer behind the wheel.

"Is that it then? Are we out of danger?" Jack Hammer asks, pulling out of the parking lot.

"Yes. For now," Digby says feeling a searing pain in his chest.

"My team is just up here on the left." Finch indicates the area sectioned off for his entourage, made up of a tour bus, electric cars and dozens of millennials holding their heads and splashing water on their faces.

"Are you sure?"

"I'll be fine, thanks to you fellas." Finch hops out of the Silver Bullet and is greeted by his assistant, who throws her arms around him sobbing with worry.

Finch appeases her concerns and gets on the phone, business as usual.

Intel is coming in from all directions at the IGA, as agents try to connect the dots of the unfolding events in Vegas. Connie, the overly ambitious junior analyst, notices Amir is not at his post. *His absence is too much of a coincidence*, she decides. She walks over to Bishop's office and sees that he's not there, as usual.

"Sir?" Connie pokes her head into Administrative Support Assistant Bill Camp's office. "The Executive Order 12333 prohibits the collection, retention, or dissemination of information about U.S. persons except pursuant to procedures established by the head of the agency and approved by the Attorney General. In this case, disseminated information for counterintelligence purposes supports national and departmental missions."

Camp looks up from his desk. "Spit it out, Connie."

"Sir, you're always emphasizing see something, say something…"

"Yes?"

"I think Amir is a terrorist, responsible for the attack on Vegas."

"Oh, good grief." Camp dials Bishop's phone. It rings on the table in the lab where Mills set it down, unanswered.

He hangs up and dials another number.

"Put pressure on the wound!" Jack Hammer screams. The sight of Digby bleeding out is causing him to drive erratically.

"We can't take him to a hospital. He's a wanted man. They'll save his life and then the Order will kill him." Mountain's voice is heavy with the bad news.

"Where to?" Jack Hammer is frantic.

"We have to get him to the Nest. I know the way."

Jack Hammer looks back to Mountain and Wabash doing their best to staunch Digby's bleeding. He flips a switch and grabs a microphone jimmy-rigged to his visor. "Well friends, what can I tell ya. The day started out like any other day. But today was the day we had to look in the face of fear and take that shot. We were right, people. This is not a drill. It got real. It got really real. This is as real as it gets. Blood has been spilled. Patriot blood. This is what you call paying the ultimate price. We're driving now to an undisclosed location. My compadres are helping the wounded. All that really comes to me is the clarity of the righteousness to this the moment. Brothers and sisters, the soil will be more fertile with our blood. We are the last line of defense. The perpetrators of our enslavement can and will be taken down but it's going to take bravery, like the bravery shown today. If you ever thought you could be a hero, in any way shape or form you take that chance. You become that hero.

You never know when that chance will come again. I'm looking at these brave faces with me right now and I'm here to tell ya, they're my heroes. So, you do what you can. Stay strong. Look into yourself. There's a hero found there. People have to stand up against our enemies. You might think that its folly to try to stand up to something so powerful, that our enemies are too great. But I ask you, if not us, who? And if not now, when? I've been called upon and I'm here to tell you, it's real. It's all real. There's strength in numbers. We are few here but there are many of you out there. Every sacrifice will make it easier. I don't know what's at the end of this road. But I know I'd rather face it with these fellas for this cause than anything else I've ever done." They pass a hip flask of whiskey around. "Thanks to the Dissidents, we're free today. To the truth! Jack Hammer out."

The MP stands firm at the gate. "I'm sorry. We cannot let him in with proper clearance."

"He's with me! I'm Joseph Bishop's daughter. It's an emergency. Call somebody!"

Leland receives a call from the gate. He turns to Bishop. "Sir, Del is here. She's brought a guest."

Bishop takes the phone. "Let them through. On my orders!"

Leland goes to retrieve them. When Del sees her father, she runs to him and throws her arms around him.

Richie is left to stand there by himself, awkwardly. When Bishop turns to him, he salutes. "Richard Wick, sir. Sorry to meet you under such precarious circumstances."

"We specialize in contingencies, son."

Richie looks around at the high-tech situation room around him. "What is this place?"

"Where good men fight for the survival of mankind."

"Dad, John's gone under."

"What? When?" Leland flashes a look of alarm. He leads the way through the maze of hallways to the lab. They find Mills laying on a gurney, eyes closed.

Del pushes past them and runs to his side. "John, you reckless idiot! Wake up!" She turns to Bishop. "I tried to call you and John answered instead. He said he was going after the source. What does that mean?"

Leland checks his vital signs.

Bishop sees his phone on the table next to John and slides it in his pocket.

Del begins to cry. "I thought you were dead all these years. Don't die again! Don't you dare leave!"

Richie watches Del react to this stranger stretched out before them and takes a step back, keeping low.

Jack Hammer pulls up to the IGA and Mountain, having been here before, instructs him to drive across the small airfield to the South Gate where the Nest is more easily accessible. Mountain does all the

208

talking. The MP calls Bishop.

"I'm clearing them. If anyone has a problem with it, they can take it up with me!"

They are directed to park the Silver Bullet in the compound's warehouse. An MP guides them to the elevator, the men carrying Digby's blood-soaked body past the IG office without being stopped. Leland meets them in the elevator and they descend to the Nest below.

Richie walks aimlessly through the main headquarters of the Amorphous Cell, watching the playback on the monitors of the people in the casino he and Del were just in, writhing in pain. He is dismayed.

Leland rushes in with Jack Hammer, Mountain and Wabash carrying Digby behind him. "To the lab!" Leland orders.

The men place Digby on a gurney and step back into the corridor as Leland desperately tries to save his life. Jack Hammer's face is tear-streamed. Mountain greets Bishop with a bear hug. The men are shaken by the unfolding events, Digby's life on the line.

Blackwell's chopper nears Paradigm Solutions. A call comes in from Bill Camp. "Sir, I think we have an internal situation here. We have reason to believe we have a homegrown terrorist on our hands. One of our junior analysts thinks she's uncovered a possible link to a terrorist plot behind the Vegas incident. I'm currently unable to get a hold of Bishop. Please advise."

"What have you gathered so far?"

"Connie, tell him what you saw." Camp pushes the speaker on the console of his phone.

"Hello, sir. It's an honor to meet you. I… I noticed a week ago Amir Chirya was looking up the schematics of the Luxor Hotel, which seemed odd because we had no directives to focus on that hotel, that location. Then, at the moment of impact, he was not at his station and nowhere to be found."

"Get me agent Dower."

"Right away, sir." Camp jumps to it.

Agent Dower enters Camp's office and sets up a small laptop on his desk. "As you know, the data is delivered over a secure API into our existing software systems. I've customized real-time data reports for asset 50631, who was stationary after his E&E until yesterday. He disappeared off the asset location map overnight, then reappeared in Vegas this afternoon, as reported earlier. But according to this…the asset is here right now."

"Here where?"

"At the IGA, sir."

"On my way." Blackwell hangs up.

Amir sits at his desk in good spirits.

Connie sees him and pulls him into a private conference room. "Where have you been?"

Amir is unable to contain his excitement. "We did it!"

"Did what?"

"I'm so sorry I've been impossible to deal with. Thank you for your patience. You're so lovely. I'd like to take you out some time, if you still want to."

"Amir, what did you do?"

"The incident in Vegas. We stopped it in its tracks. We just saved so many lives. Sorry I couldn't say anything before."

"I thought you were the one that started it! I thought you were a terrorist!"

"Connie, the first stratagem of a cover-up is disinformation. The Hegelian dialectic. If you create the catastrophe, you have the framework for guiding thoughts and actions into conflicts that lead the masses to a predetermined solution. Remember how they reported heroin overdoses in Skid Row? Those deaths were caused by disease-ridden mosquitoes developed at Paradigm Solutions. They're also responsible for the vaccines that were sterilizing people. And do you know who's behind Paradigm Solutions? B.D. Blackwell."

"Oh my God." Connie stares at him in horror. "You shouldn't be here right now. Camp couldn't get through to Bishop, so he called in Blackwell. He's on his way here. They think you and Bishop are somehow involved." She pauses, struggling with the words. "I might have overreacted and told him you were responsible. I felt it was my duty to report it. I didn't know!"

"You did what?"

"I overhead Camp talking to Blackwell. They tracked a high-level individual from Vegas to this very location." Connie's fear grows with her uncertainty. "Whoever he is, he was carrying an asset that had a military grade B360 tracking device. Full satellite communication, complete global coverage. They said he is currently here on the premises right now and considered highly dangerous. Amir, what's going on? Are we in danger?"

Amir races off to alert the Amorphous Cell. Stepping off the elevator, Amir shouts, "We're blown!" He races to the main headquarters, talking a mile a minute. "Digby had another tracker on him all along. Apparently, he's here now?"

Fu points a finger towards the lab. Amir runs to the lab and spots Bishop first. "The case has a second tracking device. Blackwell is on his way here now."

Bishop's face falls. He pulls out his phone. When the person answers, he says, "You look lovely in red."

"Oh, honey. It's happened, hasn't it."

"We'll dance under the moon soon." He hangs up.

Valentina places the phone down. *He was absent for so much of our marriage, but he's still all mine. Please keep him safe.* She turns to Bodhi and says, "Get your bug out bag, kiddo. We have to go meet Grandpa."

Bodhi looks up from his game and registers her fear. "Courage is a choice, right Grandma? You taught me that. Now we get to choose it."

Their escape plan was a part of their fabric from the beginning, something practiced. The Amorphous Cell dissembles the Nest by first scrambling all the feeds. They gather all their equipment and rig it to burn. They knew this day would one day come.

Bishop makes one last call.

Turner Boone takes out a black rotary phone from a vintage wooden cowboy chest, the only 20th century thing in his home.

"Howdy, partner."

"Can you accommodate twelve for dinner?"

"The more, the merrier. We just slaughtered a wild boar."

"We lost Matador."

"He died with honor. We can only hope someone will say that about us one day."

Bishop hangs up and addresses the group. "Leave all devices behind! And I mean everything."

They race to the nearby airstrip where an un-traceable Janet plane is on standby. They struggle to board with a comatose John in tow.

Big black commando helicopters arrive heavy. Flanked by Enforcers, Blackwell traces Digby to the Nest below. He follows the trace into the main

213

headquarters. The Amorphous Cell is nowhere to be found, the Nest gutted.

The trace leads them to the lab. Digby's dead body lies on the gurney, his case at his feet. A note is resting on his bloody chest. It reads, "You will not be punished for your anger, you will be punished by your anger." Blackwell crumples the piece of paper and tosses it on the floor, scowling.

Anchorwoman Lori Thomas adjusts the mic on her black, strappy dress. Her long blonde hair falls alongside her face in shimmery waves. "This just in. Unusually intense solar activity sent a geomagnetic storm to Earth today causing changes in the magnetic field, impacting thousands in the Southern Nevada area. Astronomers warn it's the largest active sunspot in over thirty years, launching a high concentration of solar flares in the area, releasing high-energy particles that are poisonous to humans. Normally, the ozone layer protects us from hazardous chemicals, but gradual depletion due to air pollutants from human activity called chlorofluorocarbons, some of these harmful energy particles can reach the Earth, like we saw in Vegas, and penetrate into living cells, damaging chromosomes and causing the brain to bleed. Our thought and prayers go out to all those affected by this natural occurrence. Back to you, Chip."

A picture of a panda baring his teeth lurks

behind polished anchorman Chip Heston. "Pandas. You know 'em. You love 'em. But did you know that they have an insatiable appetite for sex?"

10. THE SALLY

Amschel Rotterdam's suite takes up an entire deck, with its own private plunge pool and an infinite veranda, turning the entire living space into a sundeck.

Vanessa is trying to calm Winnie down, who is conducting a sexualized melodrama in her room. "What has gotten into you?" Vanessa asks, exasperated, fighting to put her daughter's clothes back on.

There is a knock on their suite door. A butler leads the Captain of the ship over to where Amschel is lounging in the waning sun. He notifies Amschel of an important call that just came in from Uly, his father's head nurse.

"How bad?" Amschel asks, setting his highball glass down.

"He said your father is minutes away. I'm sorry, sir."

"I'll need the Praelatus brought round."

"Wouldn't you prefer a chopper, sir?"

"No need. I'll use the time to grieve appropriately."

Amschel jettisons to Catalina Island in Praelatus, his gigayacht. A cadre of security guards meets him at the dock to accompany him to Aegis, the fortress atop the hill.

The stale air hits Amschel's nostrils as he takes his first step in the room. The curtains are drawn on all the windows, casting despair on an already gloomy environment.

Uly looks up from his console, surprised to see Amschel. He rushes over to greet him. "We weren't expecting you."

"What are you suggesting? You called to inform me he was on the verge of expiring."

"You must be mistaken. Your father is just fine. In fact, I wouldn't be surprised if he outlived us all. Would you like to see for yourself?"

The brash voice from across the room confirms sustained vigor. "Were you arriving at the eleventh hour to be my hero? Weep like a child at my bedside? Good grief."

Amschel takes small steps towards his father.

"Was that debacle in Nevada your doing? Of course it was."

"We had outside interference."

"A breach in security. Your sheer incompetence runs deep. Where is your focus, son? You say you want to run my empire, yet you can't run your own life. When you were growing up, you couldn't even dress yourself. Spoiled through and through."

"Well, I didn't ask for this."

As Amschel reaches the bed, the room goes dark. He tries to adjust his eyes.

On a picturesque hillside populated by diverse flora and fauna, Amschel finds himself on a narrow stone path up along the ridge of the cliff face, the path eroded into the peat and ropy in places. Along the ridgeline, there is a short knife-edge of rock, with steep slopes falling away on both sides. Ominous clouds devour the landscape as the sky grows dark with an impending storm rolling in beyond the sharp peaks of the surrounding mountains.

He feels a dominant presence looming. Finding a small plateau to turn carefully along a spur, he discovers the Patriarch poised at the summit draped in robes, arms outstretched and threatening, as overpowering as Zeus. The sight of him sends Amschel into a spiral. He looks down at himself and he is no longer a man but a boy of eight wearing a classic Fauntleroy suit, his purple, velvet jacket and matching knee-length pants, frilly white blouse, and floppy bow are topped with blonde ringlet curls.

His father glares at him with disgust. "You were always so much like your mother. Not hard like me."

Uly monitors the life-support machines with one eye, the other eye on a magazine. The two men silently stare at one other, motionless, the silent battle of wills taking place in their minds.

Standing in the grand entrance to their 18th century English-style stone manor, eight-year-old Amschel is calling his dog. "Jingles! Jiiiingles! Here boy!"

The Patriarch, a much younger man impeccably dressed with not a hair out of place, steps out to join him. "Jingles! Oh Jingles," he chuckles, lighting a cigar. "You know, he probably ran away because you weren't taking very good care of him. That's what dogs do, you know. They run away when they hate their masters." The Patriarch laughs and mocks the boy. "Jingles? Jingles? Where's my little Jingles? I couldn't take those sad eyes always looking at me. Those droopy, sad eyes. The two of you were made for each other."

Heavy tears roll down the young Amschel's face, his dog the only source of joy he's ever known.

"Your first and best lesson. Ultimately, the things that make us vulnerable are the very things that can harm us the most, so they need to be eliminated. I manufactured your incompetence to toughen you up. Made you strong, made you tougher. Helped prepare you for a world that would only want to take away what's rightfully yours. Taught you to never give an inch. Never care about anything. That's how we Rotterdams are. Never allow yourself to be vulnerable again."

Lightning flashes across the majestic mountainside, followed by a booming thunderclap. The Patriarch is waving his draped arms wildly through the turbulence. "You think Jingles ran away because you couldn't take care of him. That's what I told you, anyway. That wasn't it at all. It's because I killed him!"

The boy tries to put on a brave face but can't stop sobbing.

"Oh, you cried. Cried your little eyes out. Bitter tears. Whoa is me. He never ran away, I killed him with my bare hands. I killed your stupid little Jingles. Because you could never do it. Because you're not half the man I am. A state of perpetual disappointment, you are."

The grown Amschel walks the rugged path behind the boy and whispers in his ear. "No need to cry anymore. He's already full of hot air. Why not give him more of it? You have all you need to shut him up forever. Silver case. But remember, safety first!"

Amschel comes to and straightens his tie. He bee-lines for Uly, slides out the long, silver cigarette case from inside his jacket pocket, and says "Can I trouble you for the latest readout of my father's condition regarding his seizure activities? If you could print it out for me."

Uly looks up. "Sure thing." He punches some keys and as he turns to the side to retrieve it from the printer, Amchel takes out two preloaded syringes from the case, flicks them, and plunges them into Uly's neck from behind. Uly raises his arms in the air to stop him but it's too late. Amschel holds him as he begins to lose consciousness and slides off his chair and onto the floor. He grabs his wrist to check Uly's pulse. "Nasty hangover," he says while wiping his hands on his jacket and standing.

"What have you done to Uly?" Patriarch yells. He sees Amschel coming towards him and continues his tyrannical rant. "Oh, what are you going to do, grow a spine? You're not going to do anything, you floundering fool."

Amschel walks to the bedroom door and locks it. He approaches the console, moving Uly out of the way with his foot. The Patriarch is connected to a complex system that is properly vetted, the equipment fully monitored. "Since you lack a heart, father, you won't be needing this," he says, pushing a series of buttons while pulling plugs out of the wall. He sets off an alert as the generator strums on.

The Patriarch laughs at him. "The system is safeguarded from power outages. Finally, you attempt some backbone and still, you prove incompetent."

Amschel stands there, uncertain of his course of action. *You have all you need to shut him up forever.* He looks down and sees the empty needles he stuck Uly with still resting in his limp hand. He walks over to his father's bed, fills the syringes with air, and plunges them in his chest, releasing the air in the needles into his heart.

His father gasps, then continues to laugh. "You inept little scamp! You think I was hard? Your grandfather was worse. You don't know hard. But you're about to find out!" He pushes a button on his remote. The screens fill, showing the distribution of his massive wealth. "Just in case you decided to end my life, your share goes to the poor. To the poor! The ones you most loathe! You are now penniless! You inherit nothing. You are worth nothing. Not even a name. Consider your identity erased!" His heart begins squeezing the massive air emboli created from the needles, the air compressing. The bubbles block his coronary arteries, his blood flow stops, and his heart follows.

Amschel watches the Patriarch sputter and die. He quickly phones his money manager. "Sterling, check the accounts."

Sterling punches a few keys. "Sir, the strangest thing. There are no accounts. They've been wiped clean by your father."

Acting as the benefactor in his father's stead,

nothing belonged to him. He always assumed he would be taken care of. Now, frozen out of everything, he is ill-equipped to be anything by himself.

A wave up panic washes over him. He raises his arms above his head, whimpering. He turns to his father and tries to resuscitate him by pounding his chest, to no avail. He sits on the bed and tries to cry, but no tears come. He takes a deep breath, straightens his tie in an attempt to compose himself, and walks to the door. Removing two more needles from the case, he opens the door and sticks the security guard in the neck with the drugs. The security guard drops hard. Amschel takes his gun from his holster, puts it to his head and pulls the trigger. Nothing happens. *Remember, safety first!* He fumbles to find the safety on the gun, finds it, and finishes the job, leaving his brain matter splattered against the pristine white walls.

The Janet plane arrives at Cold Creek Ranch's private landing strip. Turner Boone and fellow Keepers are there to greet them.

Jack Hammer and members of the Amorphous Cell are being catered to with hot cocoa and applesauce cake, as Boone, Bishop, and Mountain sit at a round table together, glasses of whiskey in hand.

"To Digby Lange. Some give all." Mountain says. They toast.

"So, we expecting more company?" Boone asks calmly.

"Turner, I'm sorry I brought this to your doorstep."

"We all knew this day would come. I like a good romp. Keeps ya sharp."

Bishop looks at his watch. "Tina should be arriving soon."

"Oh, good. You're lucky you saw her first."

They finish their drinks in one swallow and head out to fetch her.

Wabash and Richie are in a weapons supply room.

"You were Airborne?"

"Shit nah. I do the real work. 7th Cav."

"No shit. I was 10th Battalion."

"9th."

"Hooah!"

"What do you need?"

"I ain't got enough pockets."

Wabash hands him a tactical vest and ammo.

Del sits at John's bedside. He remains motionless under a handmade patchwork quilt. When the others return, Bodhi finds her and Del jumps up to greet him, hugging him tightly. She walks him over to sit next to John's bed with her.

Leland is conferring with the Ranch's resident doctor, who speaks in a quiet, measured tone. "He has diminished Delta brain waves. There's nothing else physically wrong with him."

Bodhi can hear them in the next room. He touches his father's hand. "He's not all the way here yet. I bet I can find him." Bodhi closes his eyes.

John sits in a lotus position on the edge of a dramatic coastline formed by vertical sea cliffs, the vast expanse of the deep blue ocean in front of him, huge waves crashing against the rocks below. The pebbled beach sparkles with quartz geodes. He is skipping stones using his mind.

Bodhi ambles over and sits down next to him. John does not acknowledge his presence. After a time watching him skip stones, Bodhi asks, "What makes a good skipping stone?"

"Well, it's got to be flat. It can't be too heavy and it can't be too light. You want to try one?"

Bodhi picks up a hundred stones and skips them a thousand times.

John is amazed. "I've never seen anything like that before."

"It really is all about balance." He looks to his father. "There are so many other things I can do. Do you want to see?"

John turns and sees his son, as if for the first time. He nods his head. Bodhi reaches out his hand and John takes it. They stand up and Bodhi leads him away from the edge.

Back in the little log cabin at Cold Creek Ranch, John opens his eyes. Del rushes out of the room to summon the others.

John looks squarely at Bodhi. *Balance.*